UnLucky Double

The Adventures of

Lucky Luciano's Double

By

Darryl R. Breland

Darryl R. Breland

UnLucky Double

Copyright © 2014 Breland, LLC dba Breland Publishing, Darryl R. Breland, Managing Member. Except as provided by the Copyright Act of the United States, no part of this publication may be reproduced, stored in a retrieval system, or transmitted in any form or by any means without the prior written permission of

Breland Publishing/Darryl R Breland."

ISBN: 979-8-9866700-3-4

First Edition

Dedication

To the loves of my life,

Anna and Bailey

About the Author:

DARRYL R. BRELAND is an independent life and health insurance agent, real estate broker, developer, and a home builder from Mississippi. He writes a monthly newsletter, Your Health Matters, and has penned several articles. Recently his fiction writing hobby turned professional with the publication of UnLucky Double, a two-part series. Starlie's Tragedy to Triumph is his third book. His latest works include a series of children's books, The Adventures of Kalamazoo.

Learn more about Darryl on Facebook at @BrelandBooks or his website www.Breland.biz, and his books can be found on Amazon, Barnes and Noble, Smashwords, and other venues.

Darryl R. Breland

Contents

Acknowledgment

Special thanks to my very good friend, David Cado for allowing me to use his name for the main character. To the best of my knowledge, there has never been a Cado associated with the Mafia.

But, just in case there are some Cados in the mafia who aren't happy with this book; my name is not really Darryl Breland and I don't live in Mississippi.

Please be kind and

review this book.

Preface

Readers will have the option of purchasing *Unlucky Double* as a complete set of work, or they may purchase the book in parts. Part 1 will be offered for free or for a nominal amount in order for readers to have a taste of the subject matter and reading style before purchasing. The remaining parts will be priced based on market value.

This story is told in the first person by a fictional character who was raised in the tough Italian district of New Orleans's French Quarter during the early twentieth century. Realistically, such a character would have used less than correct language, so I hope that readers will not be offended by this realism. In keeping with this theme, history buffs will appreciate the fact that this story is intertwined with real historical facts.

My favorite historical subjects are the Mafia and World War II. Other interests of mine include time travel, possible future scientific and technological advances, politics, international intrigue, and world travel. All of these subjects are covered in this book.

It is my sincerest wish that enough people purchase this book that Hollywood will want to make a motion picture, and I will get to travel to all of the fun places described in this book as the consulting author—so buy one and tell all of your friends to buy one. Thanks in advance!

Introduction

2046 AD

The courtroom was filled with select reporters from mainstream media outlets who were known by the government for their history of favorable reporting. The prosecutor stood, waving his hand to control the hologram that helped him visually illustrate his oratory to the three judges. There was no jury of his peers for the defendant. Those days ended nearly a decade ago, as did most of the liberties that had been considered sacred by most Americans in the early years of the defendant's life.

The defendant's memory was accessed via the microchip implanted at the base of his brain, against his will, and transmitted wirelessly to a high definition, 3-D hologram. The microchip, euphemistically named the Life Enhancement Monitor, or LEM, was developed with the intention of monitoring a person's health. For example, emergency responders would be dispatched upon the first sign of a heart attack. This simple device could save millions of lives and dollars and therefore could be justified as a mandate of the Affordable Healthcare Act, imposed by an executive order. Soon, everyone in America who received government benefits of any kind was required to have the LEM implanted. In time, the majority of Americans began to accept the LEM as a way of life. More and more uses for the LEM were developed. Before long, the LEM stored all of the host's financial records and medical records, enabling a person to make financial transactions without having to carry a card or cash. More time passed, and the LEM began to be used by the criminal justice system to monitor people with criminal records and those under house arrest. Today, the LEM monitors are believed to prevent terrorist attacks and crime in general and even to control thought. The United States government points to the fact that crime is almost nonexistent thanks to the LEM. Liberty-minded ex-patriots see things quite differently.

"You are about to hear and see a fantastic tale, provided directly by the defendant's memory, that many of you will find hard to fathom; but when this trial is over, you will believe that this 147-year-old man is not a day older, physiologically, than he was one hundred years ago, and you will believe that the defendant is guilty of the charges of accessory to murder, crimes against humanity, and terrorism.

"Adolf Hitler officially died on April 30, 1945, but he didn't. Hitler escaped by submarine, carrying about fifty men to Argentina, arriving in May 18, 1945. One of those men was… is the defendant.

"On May 27, three days before his 'death,' at the stroke of midnight, Hitler ordered his team to move according to plan. The details had been planned by the head of Gestapo Heinrich Müller, right down to the clothes worn by the body doubles that would pass for the corpses of Hitler and his future bride, Eva Braun. The defendant was there. Together with Hitler and Eva Braun and others, he escaped through a secret tunnel leading away from the infamous underground bunker. The city of Berlin was on fire. Despite the explosions, they made their way to the Hohenzollerndamm in the Wilmersdorf district and from there they made their way to a boulevard that ran through the center of Berlin. A Junkers-52 transport aircraft awaiting them.

"The plane flew the defendant, the führer, Eva Braun, and others first to Denmark, then to Spain, and eventually to the Canary Islands. From there, they took a submarine to South America. About fifty people disembarked from two submarines around 11:00 p.m. on May 18, 1945, near the small port of Necochea, about three hundred miles south of Buenos Aires.

"Four men were there to greet them with pack mules and to help Hitler and the defendant cross the Andes Mountain to Argentina. They lived together in hiding at Hacienda San Ramón.

"One hundred years later, the defendant was discovered about six miles away in San Carlos de Barilche, not a day older than he was way back in 1945.

"We know this is all true, because the LEM does not allow a person to lie."

Chapter 1:
Giovani Cado

Tell us about your life, beginning with where you are from and how you became affiliated with the Mafia.

My name is Giovani Cado, but my family called me Johnny, and my friends usually just called me Cado. I was born in Sicily in 1899, so I guess that makes me one hundred and forty-seven years old. Not bad lookin' for such an old man, right?

When I was just ten years old, my father was murdered because of a vendetta or something like that. I'm not sure what that was all about, but my mother and I moved to New Orleans, Louisiana, shortly thereafter.

I loved New Orleans. My greatest desire is to return there one day, but that ain't looking so good about now. There was always a way to make an easy buck in the Big Easy. My best friend was Carlos. We made a good team, working together scamming tourists in the French Quarter. We became excellent pickpockets.

We learned at an early age that the Italian section of the Quarter was run by a man of honor, a man to respect: Don Matranga. Everybody either worked for the Don or paid him for protection.

By the time we were twelve or thirteen, Carlos and I were paid to break storefront windows of merchants who were behind in their payments to the Don.

When we were sixteen, we divided our time between making money and making it with broads. The Quarter had a steady stream of drunk gals willing to let us take a load off - drunk college gals & drunk country gals visiting the big city, and even married women whose husbands were passed out drunk or chasing other tail. Sometimes we would have two, even three different broads in one night. Then we got smart and started collecting from the husbands to find them some tail, and sometimes while they were off banging hookers, we would bang their wives. It was great.

As we got older, petty scams and picking pockets wasn't providing enough for us anymore, so Carlos and I began committing house burglaries. We would mostly steal cash and jewelry but sometimes we got lucky and would hit a house with guns too.

People began to notice us. We weren't flashy, but we spent so much time in the Quarter, seemingly without a care in the world, often with women, that locals began to speculate about how we made our living. Italians—and Sicilians in particular—who had money but no apparent job were assumed to belong to a family."

Are you referring to an organized crime family?

Yeah, that's right. Anyway, the younger boys began to make us out to be local heroes, but our reputations exceeded our real exploits.

One day, Carlos and I were hanging out down at the Flea Market, by Café du Monde, when we saw an opportunity to steal some jewelry. We went straight to this popular sandwich place called Arnaud's to divide our earnings. We sat in a booth by the window so that we could watch folks stroll by.

I can still remember that I had just ordered a shrimp po'boy and Carlos had ordered a crawfish po'boy, when we were unexpectedly joined by a couple of slightly older wise guys. They didn't introduce themselves before sitting, so Carlos, who had a Napoleon complex, being so short an' all—he was so short, that he later became known as The Little Man—anyway, he didn't like the aggressive nature of those two; sitting down with us uninvited and all.

I know—knew Carlos very well and knew that even though he was short, he was very capable of cracking those guys across their noses with our beer glasses at any moment, but I caught a glimpse of a gun holstered underneath the coat of the big burly guy sitting next to Carlos. I reached across the table and touched Carlos's forearm to get his attention. He could tell from the look I gave him that I wanted him to stay calm.

Like Carlos and me, these guys looked Sicilian. The guy next to me was first to speak: "Good afternoon Carlos and Johnny. Can we buy ya'll a beer?"

That gesture made me feel better, but I held up my beer glass to say, "Thanks, but we have full glasses."

Carlos wasn't as polite: "How the fuck do you guys know our names? And what's the meaning of this—this sitting down at our table, uninvited?"

"Allow me to introduce myself. I'm Sam, but my friends call me Silver Dollar Sam."

"I don't give a fuck if you are Samty Claus!"

But then I told Carlos in a calming tone: "Let's listen to what they have to say."

Then Silver Dollar Sam told Carlos: "You have a reasonable partner."

"OK, so what are ya, cops or something?" Carlos asked sarcastically. He knew these guys weren't cops—in fact, everyone in the quarter knew of Silver Dollar Sam. He was the Don's underboss.

The big burly guy blurted: "*You know we ain't no fucking cops!*"

Silver Dollar Sam held up a hand as if to tell the big guy to shut up and said: "No, we ain't cops, but we *do* have an understanding with the cops."

Carlos was still agitated: "Yeah, what kind of understanding?"

"Relax Carlos. We are here to make you a business proposition."

This got our attention. "We're listening," I said.

"You've attracted the attention of my boss, who has an understanding with the authorities that we can run our businesses without interference, but we don't steal from New Orleans's influential citizens. You boys have graduated from picking pockets to house burglaries, and that's bad for our business if you burglarize the wrong house."

I spoke up before Carlos could respond: "We aren't saying that we've done anything but for the sake of conversation, how could anything that we do affect your business?"

The big guy spoke again: "Because you're Sicilian, you dumb shit."

Holding his open hand up, palm facing the big guy, Silver Dollar Sam said: "Forgive my associate. He forgets that his job description doesn't include speaking…but yes, because you are Sicilian, people assume that you are part of our organization, and that means we are responsible for your actions. So the way I see it, we have two choices. You can work for us."

I asked: "What's the other option?"

Carlos answered my question for Silver Dollar Sam: "They kill us."

"We will take the first option," I said, smiling.

Silver Dollar Sam reached into the inside of his coat pocket making Carlos and me flinch. We were relieved to see that he did not pull out a gun but an envelope, which he plopped down in front of Carlos, saying: "Good choice."

Carlos and I looked at one another, each waiting for the other to reach for the envelope.

"Go ahead. Open it. The two of you decide among yourselves how to split it," Silver Dollar Sam said.

Carlos picked up the envelope and opened it. It was filled with hundred-dollar bills. He thumbed through the bills, and then asked, "What is this for?"

Silver Dollar Sam answered: "It's an advance. You now work for the Matranga family…and that means that you do what we tell you. You always look after the family's interests. No more burglaries in Orleans Parish unless you receive direct orders from me. We pay you this set amount every week; in return, you serve as enforcers. You will learn what that entails in time. You may also serve as earners. It's my job to show you the ropes. I'm responsible for you."

"There is a thousand dollars in here," Carlos proclaimed. That was more than we made in a good month.

"Monday morning…you are going to work a legit job…unloading banana boats and delivering crates of bananas around the Quarter for Sam the banana man. That will be your cover if anyone ever asks how you make your living. Got it?"

Our po'boys were delivered by the waitress. Silver Dollar Sam and the big guy stood up. And that's how we were inducted into the Mob, which you guys call the Mafia, these days.

25

The French Quarter (top)
Canal Street (bottom)
in the 1930s

Chapter 2:
The New Orleans Mafia

What was your role in the New Orleans Mafia, and how did that come about?

As instructed, we met with Sam the Banana Man that next Monday morning. He was a Russian immigrant who bought ripe bananas from the United Fruit Company and delivered them to market before they went bad. The United Fruit Company could make money selling green bananas to grocers, but ripe bananas would go bad too quickly for the grocers. The Banana Man found that he could sell the ripe bananas to neighborhood grocers in the Quarter for a bargain price and still make a profit. He made millions. In fact, he made enough money to buy his own ships to import his own bananas. He became one of the wealthiest men in the world.

We delivered bananas by day, and worked for Silver Dollar Sam at night and on weekends. At first, we followed him around officially serving as his bodyguards, but in reality we were students in Silver Dollar Sam's School for Mobsters. We learned that there was an order to things; a hierarchy, that must be respected at all times. People who stepped out of line often bought a one-way ticket to a swamp tour. I recalled how my mother had tried to prepare me to respect men such as Silver Dollar Sam and Don Matranga. Sicilian traditions carried on in America and were to be taken seriously. Silver Dollar Sam gave us small responsibilities to test our skills and decision-making abilities. We were given territories in the French Quarter to collect protection money.

We collected from every business in our territory, or "turf," on behalf of Don Matranga. It was easy because proprietors had grown accustomed to making such payments. Nevertheless, we had to get rough on some occasions. When this happened we usually notified Silver Dollar Sam and he would send a team of much bigger goons to get physical, but sometimes Carlos and I would have to do it ourselves. Carlos loved that part of the job.

Passage of the Volstead Act that prohibited the sale of alcohol changed everything for us. New Orleans and the rest of southern Louisiana did not support prohibition. The Don's clubs, gambling houses, and brothels needed alcohol to keep tourists and local patrons coming. It became our job to help keep the booze flowing in the Quarter. We also worked with restaurants, such as Arnaud's and Galatoire's, to sneak booze to them and to devise methods of hiding inventory from the rare visits by federal officers. The local police and authorities were paid to look the other way, which may not have been necessary because they were just as unhappy with prohibition as anyone…well, the Matranga family was actually happy about prohibition. Our incomes increased tenfold almost immediately in 1920 when booze could only be gotten from guys like us.

Carlos and I no longer had to collect protection money; we now had people reporting to us that did that. We made enough money that we were able to get our own apartments. I lived on Royal and Carlos had a place on Frenchmen.

Charlie's Club on Bourbon Street belonged to the Don. Strippers danced and entertained men on the first floor. Upstairs, men could go all the way, if they had enough cash.

Carlos and I met there one night after receiving a call from Joe, known as "the fisherman."

Joe explained that a patron had gotten a real beating a few weeks ago for refusing to pay after screwing one of the girls, and he had returned tonight. "He's drunk and fondling the girls, and I suspect he doesn't plan to pay his bill. I tried to reach Silver Dollar Sam, but couldn't find him, so I called y'all."

Although Carlos was known as "the little man" in the family, no one who wasn't like us—in the family that is—dared to call him that to his face. He may have been little, but he was tough and had a very short fuse. He was born in Tunisia, but he was 100 percent Sicilian and he had the temper to prove it. Because we worked for Don Matranga, people begin to say that we were connected, even made men in the Matranga family.

The truth is, we never confirmed or denied our status as made men, but it was beneficial to our health and well-being to be known that way. In fact, I never went through any type of initiation, swore an oath, or anything like that.

Only the occasional redneck tourist who had no idea what being a made-man meant dared to challenge us. We had plenty of backup too. If I had to get rough with someone, Silver Dollar Sam had a crew of enforcers that would rush to my assistance. More than a few rowdies got a real beating for stepping out of line. But we didn't have our usual backup this night, and this drunken redneck had no idea who we were. To make matters worse, he was *huge*. He looked like he might have been a riverboat hand or something like that.

I approached the big guy from behind, grabbed his shoulder, and turned him to face us. In a commanding voice, Carlos instructed him to step outside.

The belligerent redneck responded: "Who the fuck says so?" and then he raised the lower portion of his shirt to display a revolver tucked into his pants.

Carlos sprang into action by grabbing a beer bottle and smashing it over the redneck's head. People screamed and ran for the exit. The redneck drew the gun and shot off a round. He missed Carlos, but the bullet struck one of the strippers. Instinctively I tackled him. Within moments Carlos and I had disarmed and subdued the drunken man. Joe and two of the club bouncers jumped in and helped drag the redneck into a back room of the club where we tied him securely to a chair. Bound and gagged, the man remained in the back room until Silver Dollar Sam arrived.

Upon hearing the story and learning that one of his girls had been injured, Silver Dollar Sam instructed us to beat the man unconscious and then transport him to one of the Don's warehouses on Tchoupitoulas. Carlos did most of the beating and took pleasure in making the man suffer. Once the man was unconscious, Silver Dollar Sam injected him with heroin so that he would not wake on the trip to the warehouse. I hadn't seen anything like this before but I have to admit it got my adrenalin flowing. We dragged the redneck through the club and out the front door so that everyone could see what happens to those who step out of line.

Once inside the warehouse, Silver Dollar Sam had one of his men who were there waiting for our arrival place the redneck on a meat hook and then ordered one of his goons to cut him into small pieces with a saw. My excitement turned to disgust. This was the most gruesome thing I had ever seen—up until that time.

Afterward, Silver Dollar Sam ordered us to pack the bloody body parts into a crate that was loaded in the bed of a truck. Several miles outside of the city, deep into the marshes, we dug a hole where the body parts were dumped. Silver Dollar Sam had us cover the body parts in lye before the burial. Silver Dollar Sam explained that the lye helped to accelerate the process of decaying.

We were now part of the inner sanctum of the Matranga crime family, and Carlos had become the favored protégé of Silver Dollar Sam. We didn't have to deliver bananas any more.

In the days and weeks that followed, relatives of the departed redneck came to New Orleans seeking clues as to what had happened to their loved one. His name was Ted Conway. They went door to door telling everyone that he had disappeared without a trace. No one in New Orleans would dare implicate anyone connected to the Matranga family in his disappearance. The more the family searched, the more people heard about the incident. Our reputations grew as being men to respect and to fear.

Chapter 3:
Making My Bones

How did you advance in the Matranga Mafia family?

The following year, Carlos developed an idea to smuggle rum from Jamaica to New Orleans through the swampy marshes of Cajun country. The Matranga bootlegging operation was limited to distributing booze delivered to New Orleans by the Chicago outfit. Carlos shared his idea with Silver Dollar Sam, who presented the idea to Don Matranga. The Don reluctantly agreed to finance Carlos's project, which allowed him to travel to Jamaica and Chicago several times during that year. I was envious. Despite Carlos's request that I accompany him on those trips, I was ordered to keep things running in the Quarter.

Being Capo of the entire Quarter in New Orleans for the Matranga family was a lot of responsibility. The Quarter has always been the heart of New Orleans—hell, the heart of all of Louisiana, for that matter. The two biggest problems that I had to deal with were rednecks and niggers—*ouch!*

That pain in your head is the LEM reminding you that you cannot use that word. It's against the law. You may refer to African Americans as such, or you may refer to them as being black.

Oh yeah. I forgot. You've got some really fucked up laws—no, wait. Forget that. I don't need a reminder to not criticize the government. Anyway, as I was saying, Klansmen and blacks were my biggest headaches, no pun intended.

You see the city and the Mob had this arrangement. Tourism has always been important to New Orleans, and when someone gets robbed or molested in the Quarter it's bad for business. That's where the Mob came in. We could handle things in a way that the police never could.

One Saturday night, an *African American* forgot his place and came into the quarter. A confrontation with some out-of-town visitors got the attention of some of my associates, and the next thing I know I'm getting summoned to the warehouse on Tchoupitoulas. There he was, tied up, beaten up, and ready for the meat hook. Thing was, no one could find the meat hook for some reason.

It was my time to make my bones, and the guys were all looking at me. Carlos could tell that I didn't want to do it, so he instructed another man to shoot the poor black kid in the head. Carlos instructed everyone there to congratulate me on making my bones. Everyone there swore to keep our secret.

Have you ever committed murder?

No.

How did you become affiliated with the New York Mobsters?

Carlos's efforts paid off in 1922, which was an important year in our careers. Rumors circulated that Silver Dollar Sam was growing impatient with the Don's lack of ambition in the bootlegging operation and was pressuring him to step aside so the Family could maximize opportunities. Whatever the reason, Don Matranga retired and Silver Dollar Sam became the boss.

Carlos and I were officially declared top lieutenants in the family. Like I said before, contrary to local beliefs and Mafia traditions elsewhere, Carlos and I never participated in any type of ritual or swore an oath to obtain my position. It was years later, when Carlos became the boss in New Orleans, before such rituals were required of made men. He got that by copying New York families.

Before that, no one in the New Orleans Mafia needed to swear an oath of secrecy called omertà. Everyone connected knew the ramifications of being a rat. Besides, there was no one to rat to—the police and politicians from New Orleans to Baton Rouge and every small town around was either on the family's payroll or looked the other way out of fear or admiration of Silver Dollar Sam.

For this same reason, bootlegging in Louisiana was easy and virtually devoid of violence. No one objected to the brothels or gambling houses that were operated in plain view, and bootlegging was actually supported by the populace and the police. Ships carrying rum from Jamaica and Cuba would be met by speedboats just beyond the territorial waters of the United States, which was only three miles out back then. Even with a full load of cargo, these speedboats were much faster than the coast guard boats patrolling the coastline. Furthermore, the coast guard boats were piloted by men who were unfamiliar with the waters of South Louisiana, which had many twists and turns. A dead-end bayou in the marsh looks just like an open river until it just simply and suddenly ends. Virtually every structure on the bayous and river in south Louisiana served as safe houses for bootleggers.

New Orleans became *the* point of entry for most of the booze entering the Gulf Coast of the United States from the Caribbean and Latin America. New Orleans received whisky and beer from Chicago by train and riverboats Carlos and I were charged with opening new markets for our booze. Soon we were supplying nearly all of the booze that was purchased in Louisiana, the Mississippi Gulf Coast, Mobile, and the Florida Panhandle all the way to Panama City. We supplied east Texas to Dallas and parts of Arkansas with our rum.

By 1924, Carlos and I had earned more than a million dollars for the family. Of that amount, my split was about a hundred grand, which was a lot of money back then. Carlos bought an antebellum home on St. Charles in Uptown with his earnings, and I bought a home on Magazine in the Garden District. We bought our first cars.

That same year, the Don appointed Carlos as his underboss. Carlos made it a priority to promote our family's standing among Mafia bosses in New York, Chicago, and elsewhere. He brokered territorial agreements with the bosses of St. Louis and Tampa. For me personally, the most important connection he made was with Chicago's Al Capone.

Carlos arranged for Capone to visit New Orleans to see how we could expand our operations. He enjoyed the New Orleans cuisine and admired some of the gambling houses and brothels. I returned from Biloxi just in time to attend the meeting in Plaquemines Parish with Capone, Carlos, and Silver Dollar Sam. The local sheriff and two of his deputies guarded the entrance to the dirt road that led to the houseboat, where the meeting was held. Capone was impressed with our setup, especially the support from the local sheriffs and citizens.

We met at an old, run-down houseboat. When the Silver Dollar Sam, Carlos, and I arrived, we were greeted at the entrance to the long dirt road leading to the meeting place by the local sheriff, two of his deputies, and a half-dozen heavily armed guards dressed in business suits—Capone's men. The sheriff recognized us and waved us to drive through the roadblock.

Upon stepping onto the tiny houseboat, we were instructed by one of Capone's men to follow him to the other side of the boat where we met Al Capone. He was sitting in a rocking chair with his legs crossed, feet on the boat's side handrail. It was the first time I had ever been in his presence, but when he saw me Capone seemed to know me and, to everyone's surprise, called out to me: "Lucky?…What are you doing here?"

I was taken back. This was the infamous Al Capone. Even though Capone and I were the same age, he had climbed to the number two position with the most powerful crime family in Chicago. This was a much bigger deal than being the number three man in New Orleans. The outfit that Capone worked for was led by Johnny Torrio and had nearly two thousand soldiers. The entire Perini family consisted of barely one hundred soldiers. Our power over New Orleans was, in large part, the result of the misconception by many that we were much more than we were; and the exploits of men like Capone helped promote that perception in New Orleans. The story of how Capone had rigged the mayoral election in his hometown of Cicero had circulated throughout the French Quarter, especially in the Italian district. The story goes that the new mayor, once elected, publicly claimed that he was going to run Al Capone out of town, so Capone punched the new mayor in the face and knocked him down a flight of stairs in front of a crowd of reporters. The mayor never said a cross word about Capone afterward. Another tale that circulated among Italian American communities was that Capone had killed powerful, connected men, seemingly spontaneously, when he lost his temper. Supposedly, he called a meeting of his top capos and crushed one of the men's skulls with a baseball bat because he had made a mistake that Capone deemed serious.

Despite the fact that Carlos and I had witnessed gruesome murders committed by gangsters and participated in others, we were genuinely fearful of the Mafia families of Chicago and New York. We ruled New Orleans because it benefited them.

Capone seemed to be agitated by my presence, which was not a healthy situation. Instinctively, I looked behind me to see if he was addressing someone else, but there was no one else. He stood quickly, stepped past the Silver Dollar Sam and Carlos, and stood uncomfortably close to me. Carlos and I had been schooled by our Don, Silver Dollar Sam, as to the importance of showing respect to men of honor, like Capone; to always look made men in the eye, but never in a threatening way. Capone's eyes were dark, and he wasn't smiling. I've rarely been afraid of another man but I must admit this man made me nervous. This put me in a dangerous position. If I angered Capone I risked finding myself as alligator bait and if I showed my fear I risked embarrassing the family. Either way, I could be a dead man.

"I asked you a question," he repeated in his New Yorker accent.

"He's with me, Al. He is one of my most trusted men," said Silver Dollar Sam.

Capone raised his right hand, as if to say to the Don, *quiet,* yet never taking his eyes off me—he stared straight into my eyes. I realized at that moment that we—the Perini family—were small time. We had thought we were big shots, running Louisiana like kingpins, but we were really just the same punks who as kids had scammed drunken tourists visiting the French Quarter. Al Capone was big time. He could squash us like bugs. Even Silver Dollar Sam, who had deposed the feared Don Matranga, did not verbalize his objection to being disrespected in front of his men by Capone.

"What's the matter, Lucky, you can't speak for yourself?" Capone asked.

"Like the Don said; I'm with him and The Little Man— the name is Johnny Cado," I said as I offered a handshake. This is the only time that I ever called Carlos by his Mafia-given name—and later that evening he made me aware that he did not appreciate it in such a way that I never did it again.

Capone's gaze changed and he appeared a little bewildered and less agitated. "Is this some kind of fucking joke? We had an understanding that New Orleans belongs to Chicago, not New York. Is this some type of power play? And what's with this bullshit, Lucky? Why are you pretending to be someone else? And why are you talking with that fucked-up, bullshit, backwoods, redneck accent?"

"I don't know what to say, Mr. Capone, I've never been to New York," I said in a confident voice that was contrary to my true feelings.

Eager to save me, Carlos interrupted and spoke on my behalf: "With all respect, Al, he's telling the truth—I've known him all of his life. He's never been to New York."

Silver Dollar Sam, recognizing Carlos's accidental disrespect in calling Capone by his first name without permission, spoke up to save me *and* Carlos: "*Mr.* Capone, I vouch for Johnny. He is one of my men. He can be trusted."

Capone grabbed my face by my chin and turned my head to each side so that he could examine me closely. To my great relief, he smiled and said: "Well, I'll be damned. You could be Lucky Luciano's twin, except for that coon-ass accent of yours—are you related to Charlie?"

At that time, I had never heard of Charles "Lucky" Luciano and said so.

Capone stepped back and turned to the Don saying, "I believe we have a remarkable look-alike."

Then looking back at me, he said; "Lucky is too full of himself to ever call me sir or Mr. Capone. Where are you from?"

"New Orleans," I replied.

"No, where are you from, originally?" Capone asked in Sicilian.

I replied in Sicilian: "I was born in Palermo, but moved to New Orleans with my Mother when I was ten."

"Ah, very good," said Capone.

"Now that we've settled that, can we talk business?" the Don asked also speaking in Sicilian.

Capone turned to the Don and said in English, "Sure, Silver Dollar. That's what we are here for. But I have a feeling that this guy—Johnny, is it? Could be very valuable to my New York friends."

For the rest of his time with us, Capone referred to me as *Little Brother* and kept looking at me as if he were making plans for my future. As it turned out, he was doing that very thing.

Weeks later, I received instructions from the Silver Dollar Sam to meet him for dinner at one of New Orleans's finest restaurants, Galatoire's. The purpose of the meeting was a mystery to me and even to Carlos, who was the conveyor of the message from our Don, Silver Dollar Sam. My instructions were to be there at eight, but upon my arrival I was told by the hostess that my party had already been seated and that I was to join them. Seated at the table with Silver Dollar Sam and Carlos were the mayor of New Orleans, the chief of police, and two dapperly dressed men I had never seen before. There was one remaining chair, which was reserved for me.

Silver Dollar Sam smiled and welcomed me to join them: "Johnny, let me introduce you to our esteemed mayor and police chief, and two very important guests from New

York, Frank Costello, and Meyer Lansky. Gentlemen, allow me to present Johnny Cado, also known as Little Brother."

This was a strange introduction because the only person to have ever called me Little Brother was Al Capone. I shook the hand of each man, beginning with Silver Dollar Sam, then the mayor, who was dressed in an out-of-season, white linen suit, then the police chief, Colonel Molony. We didn't refer to Silver Dollar Sam as the Don in front of anyone who wasn't Italian. Next, I shook the hand of Meyer Lansky. He was noticeably short, even smaller than Carlos, had a New York Jewish accent, and looked as if he were much younger than me. Lansky continuously stared at me as if he were looking at a ghost. Equally enamored by me was Costello. He, like Lanksy, wore a dark suit and tie, but he looked more sophisticated; maybe it was because he was a few years older, maybe five to ten years older than me, or maybe it was because his pin stripes were more pronounced. At the time, I had no idea how powerful, and dangerous, these men were to become—even more powerful than Al Capone, who was already infamous, at least in the Italian communities in New York, Chicago, and New Orleans.

"Thank you for joining us for dinner, Johnny. We've been looking forward to meeting you ever since our mutual friend in Chicago told us about you," Costello said with a deep, scruffy New York dialect and a hint of an Italian accent—but not Sicilian. Then he turned to Lansky and asked: "Whaddaya think, Meyer?"

"Remarkable," Lanksy replied.

I took my seat and noticed that they had already eaten and there were three wine bottles on the table; two were empty. The waiter handed me a menu and filled my wine glass.

"Johnny, please order something to eat. We had other business to discuss before you arrived so we've already eaten, but don't let that stop you," Lansky said.

Carlos punched me on the arm and said, "You look good in a monkey suit."

"I could say the same about you," I said.

Carlos and I were street guys; as such weren't accustomed to wearing formal attire, but such is a requirement to enter Galatoire's. Then I noticed that Carlos was wearing an expensive three-piece suit—not a cheap second-hand suit like mine. I felt a sudden sting of envy and a slight feeling of betrayal. Carlos and I had grown up together as best friends and partners in crime. We were together always and had risen in the ranks together. We were thick as thieves—*literally!* Yet Carlos had been invited to attend an important meeting, from which I had been excluded, and apparently it was important to our Don, Silver Dollar Sam, for Carlos to dress as an important man—he had obviously prepared Carlos for this meeting, but he wasn't concerned if I looked like a bum.

As I studied the menu, Colonel Molony began talking. "Like I was saying, the department has thirty-three automobiles and twenty-one motorcycles—"

The Mayor interrupted him to say: "And the department was nationally recognized this year as the only one in the entire nation thoroughly equipped for first aid in all of its bureaus and precincts."

"That's all very impressive," said Lansky, but his eyes were still on me.

I placed my order; I believe it may have been veal piccata.

"I'm sorry for staring," said Lansky to me.

"Yeah, me too," said Costello.

"It's just that you bear such an uncanny resemblance to a good friend of ours—Charlie Luciano—his friends know him as Lucky. Maybe you've heard of him?" Lansky continued.

"Only once, from Mr. Ca—"

"Shhh. Let's just refer to him as our friend in Chicago," Lanksy instructed me.

"No, I'm not familiar with your friend Charlie Luciano," I replied.

Silver Dollar Sam politely explained to the mayor and the police chief that their business had concluded and that he had other matters to discuss with his guests from New York. The men thanked him for the delicious meal and for introducing them to Mr. Lansky and Mr. Costello. As they shook hands, Costello said to the mayor: "We will discuss Mr. Perini's proposal with our partners, and if there is no conflict between our thing in New York and our agreement with the outfit in Chicago, we would be happy to work with you all in New Orleans." My dinner was delivered just as the mayor and chief departed.

Lansky leaned forward with his elbows resting on the table and asked me: "Johnny, pardon me for asking, but how tall are you?"

"I'm five feet, ten inches. Why do you ask?"

Lansky explained that he was planning to have a party on New Year's Eve and wanted me to come as his surprise guest, dressed as a Lucky Luciano look-alike. Silver Dollar Sam and Carlos were invited as well, but he made it clear that we were to tell no one because he wanted to surprise Lucky and the other guests with my appearance. Costello gave me a pen and note pad and told me to write down my clothing sizes so that they could have my wardrobe custom tailored to fit me. My envy of Carlos was beginning to wane, as Lanksy and Costello made me feel as if I were important.

Al Capone

Lucky Luciano

Chapter 4:
The New York Mob

Tell us about your first trip to New York. I believe it was on the eve of 1922.

Frank Costello delivered the clothes that I was to wear to the party. Just as the barber was putting his clippers away, Costello removed a bill from his wallet, handed it to the barber and said: "Remember, not a word to anyone about this—to anyone."

The barber nodded, acknowledging that he understood. Costello knew that Luciano's long-time barber could be trusted. The barber collected his bag and left my hotel room. With this haircut, I now looked more like Lucky Luciano than ever before, according to Costello.

The clothes were custom tailored for me to match Lucky's wardrobe. Costello reminded me of my instructions; chief among them was to "say almost nothing to anyone other than me—not even to Silver Dollar Sam or Carlos. If you have to speak, do so in Sicilian and sound as if your voice is strained. The story is that you are recovering from the flu and you've lost your voice."

Costello was concerned about my accent. It was apparent that I looked like Lucky Luciano, the guest of honor, but I sounded nothing like him. "You sound like you *might* be from Boston, but definitely not New York," said

Costello, who was clearly an Italian-born New Yorker. "And, don't drink too much."

My instructions were to get dressed and wait for Costello to return to my room, so that he could escort me to the party downstairs in one of the Knickerbocker's grand ballrooms.

Costello returned just before ten o'clock to accompany me to the party. Two tough-looking men stood guard in the hall, limiting access to my hotel room. Costello reminded me once again, "Remember, you are Lucky Luciano, who will be meeting Silver Dollar Sam and Carlos for the very first time tonight. Your best friends, besides me and Meyer Lanksy, are Vito Genovese, Albert Anastasia, and Ben Siegel. And whatever you do, do *not* make the mistake of calling Ben by his nickname Bugsy. They don't know that you aren't the real Luciano, so act as if you are glad to see them and everyone else but don't say nothing to none of them. The only person, besides me and Meyer, that will be there who knows that you are not Lucky is Arnold Rothstein. I will point him out to you. Arnold is a big cheese and is the only one who tells Lucky what to do. The three of us, Arnold, Meyer, and me, will keep you from having to talk."

The elevator doors swung open to the ballroom level. This was the grandest event that I had ever experienced. The fur coats, diamond rings and necklaces, and the gold watches—New Orleans was the wealthiest city in the south, but the money dripping off of people in this place surpassed anything that I had ever seen. There were at least one hundred people in the place. In addition to the dapper dons and elegant ladies, there were scantily clad flapper girls, ice sculptures, balloons, confetti, and musicians.

Several people acknowledged us as we walked by, but as instructed I did not stop to speak to anyone. Costello and I stopped walking, and he directed my attention to the round table only a few steps away where Lansky was sitting with three men that I had yet to meet. Speaking softly in Italian, he briefly explained who each person at the table was and their relationship with Lucky.

Extending his hand to shake mine, Arnold was the first to speak: "I'm sorry to hear about your laryngitis, Lucky. You must have gotten hold of some rotten hooch, likely from Dutch." This generated a few chuckles. Arnold was the oldest among the group, and the most famous. He was well known as a multi-millionaire business man and gambler. He was less known, at least publicly, as a gangster and bootlegger. Arnold was known by the Mob as *The Brain*, because he was a brilliant schemer. He was an exquisite dresser and eloquent speaker. He taught Lucky how to dress in the way of high society, silk shirts and silk ties and all. Ben Siegel and Frank Costello emulated Lucky's new dapper style which resulted in creating the stereotypical image of the well-dressed Italian Mobster.

Ben Siegel added to the laughter by saying, "Bad *cooch* is more like it." Ben was a handsome, but brutal man. He was a lover and a fighter. Lucky first met Ben as a teenage street thug and Lansky's sidekick. In public, he was seen most often with a beautiful woman by his side, but he was a feared Mafioso with a reputation for killing first and asking questions later.

"Now, now, Arnold; we have an understanding that Dutch will not be selling any more of his product in our territory, and to let bygones be bygones," said Lansky, smiling, as he shook my hand. "Happy new year, Lucky."

Lucky first met Meyer Lansky when they were barely teenagers. The story goes that Lansky, despite being much smaller, refused to pay Lucky for protection; a common racket among Italians. Lucky respected Lansky and they became best friends. Lucky was the first Sicilian gangster to accept a Jew as his equal. This has had major implications for the development of the Mafia because Lansky introduced Lucky to Arnold Rothstein who taught the young Italians to organize their criminal efforts. In time, Lansky replaced Arnold as the brilliant criminal mind that directed the Italian Mafia to become the national crime syndicate.

The man named Dutch Shultz did not laugh or reach for my hand to shake. Instinctively, I turned to shake his hand next, but Costello indiscreetly used his hand to keep my arm from extending in Shultz's direction and pulled out a chair for me to take a seat. Without having to be asked, a waiter was quick to pour a drink for me and Costello.

In a more serious tone, Arnold said: "Yes Meyer that *is* in the past. Thank you for reminding me. Mr. Shultz, if there is nothing else, I would like to discuss some things with my associates now that Lucky and Frank are here."

"Certainly. Happy new year to all of you," Shultz said, looking directly at me as he stood to leave.

I noticed that Costello and Lansky seemed to be fighting to keep from laughing out loud at how everyone was fooled by Lucky's double. Costello had a scratchy voice as the result of a botched tonsillectomy. He had broad shoulders and was also popular with the ladies. When Costello was younger, he carried a gun and wasn't afraid to use it, but by this time, he used his uncanny ability to develop relationships with politicians, judges, and the police to benefit the Mafia.

Rothstein raised his glass. "May I be the first to toast to a prosperous New Year?"

"Even more prosperous than this past year," said Meyer raising his glass.

The other glasses were raised and clinked together. Then Lansky said to me: "Lucky, don't try to talk, because I don't want you to strain your voice so that you can recover faster—"

"*No!* I think I like him better without a voice!" Ben interrupted. We all laughed but some of us weren't laughing at Ben's joke—we laughed because Ben still thought that I was the real Lucky Luciano. This was especially interesting because, I had learned, Ben "Bugsy" Siegel and Lucky Luciano had been close friends since they were teenage street thugs. In fact, no one was closer to Lucky, other than Meyer Lansky and Frank Costello.

"As I was saying, just nod your head," Lansky continued. "Do you think that Ben will ever settle down with one woman?"

I shook my head, side to side, just as I had been coached.

"I can say the same about you, pal," Siegel said as he raised another glass in the air, motioning it in my direction.

We all laughed; again it was the situation, not Siegel's remarks, that caused the laughter.

"Ben, do you know any new jokes?" asked Costello.

"You know I do." Ben told a few jokes. I don't recall the content, but we laughed and laughed.

The laughter caught the attention of another Italian who I learned later to be Tommy Lucchese, and he joined our table, sitting in Dutch Shultz's vacated chair. He waited for Ben to finish his latest joke so that he could contribute his joke.

Tommy was proud of himself for the laughter that his joke generated. He then stood with glass raised and said, "To the Volstead Act!" But before anyone downed their drink, Costello said: "You've made that same toast for the past two years; how about something new."

"All right! To a happy new year, and to not taking too big a bite!"

After Tommy left our table, Lansky got everyone's attention: "Gentlemen, I propose that we move our group up to Lucky's suite for a special presentation. Frank, would you see to it that Silver Dollar Sam and Carlos join us there?" Vito Genovese and Albert Anastasia were instructed to remain at the party.

The rest of us followed Lansky's instructions and made our way through the ballroom. Along the way, I received many smiles and winks from the ladies. There were two armed guards sitting in chairs on each side of the door to Lucky's suite, just as I had seen outside my room. We entered the suite, past the guards. Lansky instructed everyone to sit and drink until Costello arrived with Silver Dollar Sam and Carlos so that he could make the presentation to all of us at once. We did exactly as we were told.

Seated with me were Carlos, Sam, Rothstein, Costello, and Siegel. Lansky was the only one standing as he spoke: "Gentlemen. I have something extraordinary to present tonight. Lucky, would you please walk over to me."

As instructed, I stood up and walked over to Lansky. Seconds later, the real Lucky Luciano entered the room and walked up to me. Luciano looked at me with amazement, and I at him. It was as if we were looking at ourselves in a mirror. I realized now why Costello had selected the clothes that I was wearing. The real Lucky was wearing identical clothes from hat to shoes. Ben Siegel was the most surprised of all for he was the only one in the room previously unaware of my existence, besides Lucky. For this reason, Lansky selected Ben Siegel to guess which one of us was the real Lucky Luciano. He guessed correctly but only after closely studying us—and even then he wasn't totally confident in his decision. What gave it away, he said, was "the eyes—Lucky is surer of himself, and it shows in his eyes."

Lansky stressed that my existence should remain top secret. "It could be very useful to our thing for Lucky to have a double. No one outside of this room knows about Little Brother—and we are to keep it that way."

"Except for Al Capone," Carlos said.

"I've already handled it with Al," Lansky replied.

"As I was saying, this is top secret information. *No one* is to speak of this to *anyone* outside if this room—Ben, no one—not to Vito, not to Albert or Tommy—" Lansky continued.

"Yeah, I get the picture," said Siegel. "Nobody."

Luciano took charge. "Now that we've settled that, I would like to spend a few minutes getting to know my look-alike. Enjoy the rest of the party and I will be down in a few. Ben, send a couple of playthings up for Little Brother in about thirty minutes."

Everyone left the room except for Lucky, Lansky, and me. The three of us sat in the living room of Lucky's suite, each with a drink in our hand. Lucky asked a lot of questions about my history. He wanted to know about my family, which was limited to my mother who lived in New Orleans, and her sister and her sister's husband and their children, all of whom lived in Sicily, and whom I had never met. My mother never wanted to discuss them. Lucky spoke mostly in English, but he occasionally spoke Sicilian. When he did, I reciprocated by speaking in Sicilian. Lansky said that we sounded far more similar when we spoke in our native tongue. After a short while, Lucky told me that he wanted me to work for him and Lansky. "Silver Dollar has already agreed, but the ultimate decision is up to you." He explained that he and Lansky were hatching a plan that could benefit from having me to serve as a decoy, or alibi, for Lucky. Accepting his offer meant that I would have to spend a great deal of time in hiding, for no one could know of me other than his most trusted circle of confidants. "Loyalty is as important as life and death," he explained.

"What's in it for me?" I asked.

Lucky and Meyer took turns explaining how I would be taken care of for the rest of my life. I would have enough money to do anything that I wanted; I could open my own business or travel the world. "But, for the next four or five years, we will need you to live a very quiet life—nothing dangerous and never in the spotlight. After all, you break a bone and have to wear a cast, I have to wear a cast." Lucky explained.

Then Lucky pointed out that he had enemies. "If they were to mistake you as me, it would be best if you have our protection. There is a reason that I have armed guards outside of my door around the clock." They told me that I didn't have to decide right away, so we agreed that I would stay in New York for a month and see how it went.

There was a hotel room with a connecting door to Lucky's suite. Lansky had a professional special effects guy design a costume that Lucky and I would take turns wearing. I was never to leave my room without wearing the disguise, unless I was supposed to be Lucky; in which case, he wore the disguise. A voice and acting coach was hired to teach me how to walk and talk like Lucky. After a few weeks, I was subjected to a series of tests. I would have dinner in a public place with one of Lucky's gals or pals. If anyone approached me to speak, his pals would intercede on my behalf, or I would speak in Italian.

After a month of this, it was an easy decision. I could have anything I wanted delivered to my room. Steak, lobster, and champagne every night of the week if I wanted, and I had my pick of beautiful women, sometimes two and three at a time. When I got stir crazy, Lucky would arrange for me to have a vacation far away from New York, where no one was likely to recognize Lucky. Over the next four years, I got to visit Bermuda, the Bahamas, and Miami, among other places. All that I had to do was to be seen somewhere in public when it benefited Lucky, so that he could be somewhere else without his enemies knowing. Lucky was arrested several times and subsequently released, because credible witnesses would swear that they saw him far away from the scene of the crime while the crime was occurring. Once I spent a week in Hot Springs, Arkansas, pretending to be Lucky Luciano. I was a real celebrity among the locals. They loved for mobsters to visit their little town.

By 1929, Lucky had been using my services for a couple of years, at least. I would meet hoodlums on rooftops and even in Central Park to swap a briefcase of unknown contents for another briefcase of unknown contents. During these swaps, I would almost always speak in Italian, but by now, I could mimic Lucky's English. This special arrangement had gone very well for Lucky and me, but one night things went terribly wrong. I was having dinner with Ben Siegel and a couple of beautiful broads at this really good Italian restaurant called Delmonico's. I was approached by Tommy Luca, who I knew to be one of Salvatore Maranzano's men. He pretended to be Lucky's friend, but we all knew that he was a double agent. Don Maranzano was a dangerous rival to Lucky's boss Don Masseria.

"Lucky, I'm surprised to see you here. I had heard you were in Brooklyn tonight."

I had been well coached and knew how to respond to almost any situation. In English, I said: "I've been here all night with my pal, Ben, and my gal Erika."

Tommy responded in Sicilian. "Right now in Brooklyn Don Maranzano is meeting with someone who looks an awful lot like you."

I replied in Sicilian: "He has discovered my secret double. Please keep my secret, as it has given me plenty of alibis when I've needed one."

This saved Lucky's life. At that moment, he was being given a severe beating by Maranzano, but Lucky claimed that he was me, the look-alike, and that I was the real Lucky Luciano. Tommy Luca made a call to Maranzano and convinced him that he was certain that the real Lucky Luciano was having dinner at Delmonico's.

Although I saved Lucky's life that night, this was the beginning of the end of our mutually beneficial relationship.

Darryl R. Breland

The Waldorf Astoria

(home of Lucky Luciano)

1930s to 1940s

Chapter 5:
Biloxi, Mississippi

What happened to sour your relationship with Luciano?

Well, first of all, since the word was out among his enemies that I existed, it was decided that I should retire from the role of being Lucky's double for a while. So I returned to New Orleans with instructions to lay low. Upon my return, I was told that Silver Dollar Sam had learned from the New York Mafia how organized crime should be managed. Unlike the Matranga Family, the Perini Family was more structured and disciplined. No one, other than Carlos, had access to Silver Dollar Sam anymore; and no one other than top lieutenants, like me, had access to Carlos—only capos and lieutenants could talk to one another, and so on. There was no way to be sure, but I suspected that the Perini family took orders directly from the Masseria family of New York—specifically Lucky Luciano.

There was a turf war raging in New Orleans at that time between the Perini family and an Irish gang led by William Bailey. Lucky wanted to make certain that I wasn't involved in anything that could risk altering my appearance because he wasn't sure if he was through with me yet, so Carlos ordered me to manage a gambling operation that was located in a beachside hotel in Biloxi.

This was a boring assignment until I met Melissa. She was the most beautiful woman that I had ever seen—the kind that looks good first thing in the morning without any makeup. She had an exciting personality but was wild and crazy—certifiably crazy. We had a connection right away, but I was definitely more into her than she was into me. After I grew to know her I understood that she had issues that kept her from feeling attachment or trusting anyone, particularly men. As a result, we had a rollercoaster relationship. She would tell me one day that she loved me and wanted to spend the rest of her life with me as my wife, but the next day she would tell me that she did not want to be in a relationship of any sort with anyone. In spite of that, we became good friends. She often said that no one had ever treated her better or respected her more than I. Her flirtatious nature gave her an unflattering reputation, but there was no doubt in my mind that I was in love with her. I had reconciled to continue having a romantic courtship with periodic interruptions in the hope that she would eventually come to terms with her issues and make a permanent commitment to me.

Carlos rarely called anyone on the telephone, especially if it regarded the family business, but he made an exception this one particular day. He called to tell me that everyone, including me, was required to be in New Orleans right away for important business. I made the mistake of telling Melissa where I was going because she insisted on going with me. She loved New Orleans with a passion. It was difficult to disagree with her. That evening, we checked into the Monteleone and took in the wonderful sights of the city. It was a strange experience for me. This was the first time that I had ever experienced New Orleans as a tourist, and not as the life-long native that I was. I don't recall having more fun before that.

Duty called the following day. Everyone in the Perini family was instructed to meet at the train station, which was surrounded by three or four hundred Italians; many were wielding baseball bats or iron bars. A capo recognized me and instructed the crowd to part to allow me to move through the crowd and depot to the landing deck. Silver Dollar Sam was there, which was a rare site indeed. Next to him were Carlos and a team of uniformed police officers. Upon seeing me, Carlos approached and instructed me to move far enough away that I would not be involved if things got rough.

An arriving train, its whistle blaring, came to a stop; out came Al Capone and his men. Silver Dollar Sam ordered the police to disarm Capone and his men. They did. Capone was furious and made it known by pointing his finger at Silver Dollar Sam as if it were a gun and emulating the pulling of a trigger. Silver Dollar Sam responded by ordering the police to break the fingers of Capone's men, which is what happened next. Seeing the huge crowd, Capone realized it was useless to fight back. He ordered his men to restrain themselves and not to fight back. It was an unusual sight: policemen breaking the fingers of well-dressed goons who refused to cry out in pain. Capone and his injured men returned to Chicago on the next train and never returned to New Orleans. It was obvious to all that New Orleans was now controlled by New York and not Chicago.

Later that year, the stock market crashed. Our gambling business suffered as a result. Like for many others, times were tough for me. Unlike all of the other lieutenants, I had no capos or crews reporting to me. That meant the only income that I had was my take from the rinky-dink, redneck casino that I ran for the family. Unfortunately, the family decided to turn over the casino to the hotel owner at the end of the year and abandon our interests. It simply costs more to manage than it made for the family. The good news was that I was going to return to New Orleans. The bad news was that Melissa would not commit one way or the other to moving with me. One day she wanted to sell her house and move away with me; the next day she would change her mind.

Despite that, Melissa and I celebrated New Year's Eve at a party hosted by Silver Dollar Sam in New Orleans. It was a lavishly tacky event. Melissa had no idea that I had ties to the Mob. In those days, the term "Mafia" was little known and rarely used. Average people, such as Melissa, had no idea that criminal activities were organized. She was, however, perceptive in noticing that something was peculiar about this crowd. How could anyone help but notice how everyone seemed to pay homage to Carlos and even more homage to the Don, Silver Dollar Sam Perini? There was a clear hierarchy in place.

In reality, I was a lieutenant in name only but the title earned me respect, and Melissa could not help but notice that lower-ranking Mafioso paid homage to me as well. This became problematic a few months later when I began to deplete my savings. Her impression was that I was much more important and well-off than I really was. She had remained in Gulfport all of this time using the fact that she had to sell her home first—one that she had inherited from an ex-husband. The more I began to tighten my belt, so to speak, the more uncertain she became about moving to New Orleans and committing to a future with me. In the end, she remained on the coast.

Carlos agreed to hire me to be his right-hand man; my title remained unchanged. This meant having bodyguards protecting me around the clock. This impressed Melissa. She felt sure that I was really important, so I must be rich. The irony is that the bodyguards were paid more than me. Carlos had agreed to hire me simply as a friend, but the Perini family had strict orders from Luciano to keep me safe. If I were going to keep Melissa happy, I must find a way to make more money. The bootlegger war with the Bailey family was nearing an end but wasn't over, so Carlos simply could not afford to have me involved with anything dangerous, which meant there was very little money involved in the various safe operations that I was assigned to. These guys are not the sort of people you should complain to about anything; especially money, but I needed a job.

By spring of that year, I was desperate. Melissa was avoiding me by making excuses for not visiting me in New Orleans. Then Frank Costello called to tell me that I was being requested to return to New York for a potential job. Maybe this was my *lucky* break—no pun intended. The problem was, that I couldn't tell anyone other than Carlos and Sam that I was going to New York, not even Melissa. She was a real bitch when I gave her the story that I was going away for a long time on a business trip without her to South America. This was the life that I chose and once in the Mob, there is no getting out—alive, that is.

Biloxi, Mississippi in the 1930s

The French Quarter today

Frank Costello

Meyer Lansky

Chapter 6:
Deep inside the Mob

Perini family bodyguards escorted me to New York, but Lucky's people took responsibility for my security once I got off the train at Grand Central Station. There to meet me were Frank Costello, Ben Siegel, and Albert Anastasia. Prior to my trip, I had been given instructions on exactly what clothes to wear, in case anyone saw me and mistook me for the real Lucky.

Costello and I rode in the back seat of a car that was being escorted by two others—one in front of us and one following. Albert rode in the first car, and Ben rode in the car that followed. There were four men in each car, which meant that a total of eleven men escorted me from the train station to the Waldorf Astoria. The Mob isn't into impressing people, so this much security must have meant that something big was happening in New York.

I was allowed to rest that evening and all of the next day, but I was not allowed to leave my room. There were two guards positioned outside of my hotel room. Since none of Lucky's enemies could possibly know that I was in that room, it was apparent that they were there to keep me in, not to keep others out.

The afternoon of the following day, I was visited by Costello and Lansky. Costello led the discussion by reminding me how we had agreed that if something happened to me—for example if I broke my leg—that the real Lucky would have to wear a cast to make sure that no one could tell us apart.

Lansky asked me if I recalled that conversation and I confirmed that I had. "Well, that's great, because we have something to show you."

They led me to Lucky's suite, which was on the 39th floor of the Waldorf Towers, but on another hall, just around the corner from my room. Lucky was sitting in a chair looking straight ahead providing me with a profile view of his face. It was strange how he did not stand, or even turn his head to face us as we walked into the room, or when he spoke to me:

"Welcome back to New York, Little Brother."

Then he turned to face me. That is when I noticed that one of his eyes drooped. He turned his head more so that I could see the other side of his face. There was a long L-shaped scar that had not been there before.

"Oh shit. What happened, Lucky?" I asked.

"This is from that night that you ran into Tommy at Delmonico's," he replied as he gestured to the scar. Then he instructed me to sit down on the sofa across from him. "That was months ago, and it has already begun to heal. We will need your services again soon, so we need for you to have the same scar and the same droopy eye." He could tell by the look on my face that I was horrified. "Don't be scared. Unlike me, you will be under anesthesia and under the care of a professional doctor." He motioned to Costello to pour me a drink, which he did. Lucky then went on to explain to me that the choice was mine: I could decline but if I agreed, there would be a hundred grand in it for me.

In today's money, that's like three or four million dollars. I downed my drink and thought of Melissa, wondering if it would affect her feelings for me. Hell, I wasn't sure if she had any feelings for me anyway, so of course, I would do it, but such a big decision deserved serious thought, so I asked if I could sleep on it.

Lucky laughed and said: "Of course, you can sleep. Go ahead, lie down on the sofa, and sleep right now."

Within seconds, my eyelids felt heavy, and just before I fell asleep I could hear the others laughing. When I woke, I was lying in Lucky's bed, with an I.V. drip attached to my arm, and could see out of only one eye. I had been drugged. I took my free hand and felt the bandages on my face. *Those sons of bitches;* they hadn't given me a choice. If they had, I am almost certain that I would have agreed to it, but that wasn't the point; they did this to me without permission. I was pissed but smart enough not to show my anger to any of those wise guys.

The first visitor, other than the doctor and his nurse, was Silver Dollar Sam. He came to New York to tell me that he was proud that one of his men, a member of his family, was chosen for such an important job and was so brave to make this sacrifice. He assumed that this had all been voluntary. "You will be on easy street from this day forward. Here, take this as my token of appreciation."

The envelope that he handed me had five grand. Of course, I thanked him but I wondered if this was it. Would I see the hundred grand that I was promised by Lucky? I dared not ask, yet.

Later that day, I was visited by Lucky. He thanked me for my loyalty and sacrifice but made a point of telling me how much more pain he had to suffer to obtain the same scar. "They beat me until they thought I was dead. I wanted to be dead."

Was he telling me that I should be thankful?

"You will remain here in this room, part of my suite; you will be cared for and looked after until you have recovered. Anything you want, just ask for it," he said.

Hindsight is twenty-twenty—I should have asked, "How about the hundred grand that you promised, you asshole?" but I didn't.

A few days later, I read where Silver Dollar Sam had been arrested in New Orleans for the shooting death of a federal narcotics agent. That was impossible; he was in New York visiting me the day of the murder. Unfortunately for Silver Dollar Sam, neither I nor any of the Luciano gang could serve as witnesses, and he was convicted and served two years in jail for that murder. Carlos became acting Don of the Perini family in Silver Dollar Sam's absence.

As the weeks went by, Lucky was very creative in finding ways to keep me happy. Breakfast was served to me in bed, typically by a scantily clad stripper, who would pop my top, if you know what I mean, as soon as I finished my eggs Benedict and mimosas. One morning I was awakened by a beautiful, young, busty redhead with her head underneath my covers. I was offered drugs, heroin, cocaine, marijuana, whatever I wanted, but I refrained from all of that stuff; just alcohol for me.

In time, I fully recovered and was allowed to exercise. At first, I was limited to the hotel gym, but eventually, I was driven, clandestinely, to upstate New York to live in a hillside cabin. I missed Melissa, so without asking for permission I called her. She acted as if she hardly knew me. There was no "I'm so happy to hear from you; I missed you." None of that; I was so disappointed.

A year and a half later, I was going bat-shit crazy alone in the fricking woods. I had had too much time to think about Melissa and about the hundred thousand dollars that I still had not received. I grew more bitter. My anger was directed mostly toward Lucky, but I was bitter at everyone who was in that room the day that I was drugged, laughing as I dozed off. Who was there? Let's see, Costello was there; he was the bastard who gave me the drink. Lansky was there. I think Ben was there. Yeah, I think I remember hearing him laugh. Was Vito or Albert there? The more I thought about it, the more certain that I was that Vito was not there. I started thinking about revenge. Those are dangerous thoughts when we are talking about mobsters. Vito, Albert, and Ben belonged to a group known as Murder, Incorporated, for good reason.

It was the fall of 1931 before anyone from the Mob visited me again at the cabin. Three men arrived in one car. The driver got out and opened the door for the man riding in the back, and the other man in the back got out and stood by the car. The driver returned to his place in the car, and the third man, the one riding in the back of the car, walked toward the cabin, where I was standing on the front porch.

It was Frank Costello. That fucker; I wanted to stab him in the eye with an ice pick.

"It's time for you to return to New York. We have a job for you to do."

Back at the Waldorf Astoria once again, waiting for me in Lucky's room were Lucky and Meyer. Frank and I entered the room and sat, as instructed. Lansky sat there quietly without saying a word; Lucky did all of the talking. First, he asked a lot of meaningless small-talk questions. My life had been one boring monotonous day after another for a long time. My tact and patience had worn thin, so I told Lucky bluntly that I had been cooped up so long that I had nothing interesting to talk about and that I needed action and needed to make some money.

"Well today is your *lucky* day," he said, with pun intended. He reached his hand into his inside coat pocket and drew out a stack of hundred-dollar bills. He laid it on the table in front of me. "Here is one hundred thousand dollars. Follow my next instructions to the letter, and it will be here for you when you return."

For a fleeting moment, I considered grabbing that stack of money, which already belonged to me, and trying to make a run for it—but then the image of me hanging from a meat hook, with Frank Costello beating me and Vito Genovese holding a chain saw, popped into my head, and so I quickly forgot that foolish notion and listened to his instructions.

Costello and two bodyguards led Lansky and me down to the lobby of the Waldorf. As we walked, it occurred to me that Lansky had yet to speak a word, which was highly unusual, so I cordially asked how he had been.

Costello said in a stern tone: "Don't talk to him before you are together, alone in the car."

Lansky and I were in the back seat of the car with only a driver in the front seat. I looked at him and said, "That's odd. There have always been two guys in the front seat. A driver *and* a bodyguard."

Then Lansky looked at me and said, "I'm not Meyer."

After a few seconds of absorbing what he had just said, I asked for clarification.

"I'm not Meyer Lansky. I'm his double, just like you are Lucky's double. My real name is David. That's all that I am allowed to tell you about myself."

The driver turned his head somewhat, trying to listen to our conversation.

"What does this mean?" I asked.

David whispered his theory, which was that we were being used as decoys; there was a hit out for Lansky and Lucky, and the hit man was Mad Dog Cole. The plan was to use the two of us as bait so that Lucky's men could lie in wait and catch Mad Dog Cole in the act of trying to kill us.

"Geez, we are fucking targets?" I asked.

The driver suddenly parked the car in front of a corner store, turned to us, and said, "I will be right back." Then he exited the car. I looked at David and he looked at me; both of us knew that something was wrong. I grabbed David by the neck and pulled his head down toward me and yelled, *"Get down!"* and I did the same. No more than a couple of seconds prior to that, I had seen a man in a car next to our parked car holding a Tommy gun. We ducked just in time to miss the first shots. Instinctively, I opened the car door on my side, which was on the opposite side from the shooter. I fell out onto the sidewalk and David, the Lansky look-alike, crawled out also, landing on top of me. The shooter must have fired a dozen shots into the side of our car before his car raced away.

Before David and I could get to our feet, a photographer appeared in time to snap our picture. While we were still recovering from the bright flash of light, Frank Costello and Ben Siegel appeared on the scene.

They both called out the names of Charlie Luciano and Meyer Lansky so that everyone could hear and believe that we were them. "Come with us, quickly," Costello ordered.

David and I followed Costello and Siegel without showing our reluctance, but we were both certain that the Luciano-Lansky gangs considered us expendable. The photographer who was on the scene was there, in my opinion, to take pictures of dead bodies for the newspaper, so that the Maranzano gang would think they had won the war against the Masseria gang.

We were ushered up to Lucky's suite where he and Lansky were waiting. It was a bizarre moment. Lucky

Luciano and Meyer Lansky sitting directly across from David and me; it was as if were talking to ourselves. I'm not sure if was the adrenaline or what, but I had a lot more confidence to speak my mind. Quite frankly, I felt that if they were trying to kill me I didn't have anything to lose. So I made it clear that I was pissed about being set up to be a sitting duck for a hit man, pissed that I hadn't received my hundred grand, pissed that my face had been butchered without permission, but most of all I was pissed because I had to spend the last year and a half as a recluse in the middle of nowhere, which had cost me my relationship with Melissa. I had had enough of this bullshit!

David, the Lansky look-alike, did not back me up. He sat there like a scared wimp.

Lucky and Lansky surprised me with how calmly they reacted to my losing my temper and speaking my mind. Lucky stood up and left the room without saying a word, while Lansky tried to assure us that they had no idea that we were going to be the targets of a hit, but I no longer believed him. Lucky returned with a brown leather satchel, handed it to me, and said, "See? Here is your money. We weren't trying to cheat you. We are men of honor. We've built our entire business by keeping our word."

It was hard to argue that point. One thing the Mob had a reputation for was honoring contracts, which were never in writing, of course. My money was there, all hundred grand.

David asked: "What about me?"

"We will take care of you later," Lansky replied just before rising from his chair. He opened the door and instructed a guard to escort David to his safe house. I never saw the Meyer Lansky look-alike again.

The money made me feel much better, so I apologized for my outburst and lack of confidence in them and expressed my gratitude for the payment. Of course, it would have been nice to have had it a year and a half before.

Lucky responded by assuring me that there were no hard feelings and went on to say that his men had captured the would-be assassin, Mad Dog Cole. "Thank you for your service." The best news of all was that they would not need my services for the time being and that I was free to return home.

Their bodyguards were assigned to escort me back to New Orleans, for my safety. I have to admit I remained distrustful of those guys and was paranoid that I was going to be put on ice before I had a chance to spend any of this hard-earned money. Before going to the train station, my "bodyguards" agreed to stop at Tiffany's, where I purchased a three-carat diamond engagement ring to give to Melissa.

The journey home was stressful because I felt as though I might be thrown from the train if I gave the men the opportunity. But once I returned to Biloxi and learned that Melissa had married another man I wished that those men had killed me. Out of anger, I walked to the end of a pier and tossed the ring into the Gulf of Mexico. I regret that stupid, impulsive act, but I have no regrets at all about my next impulsive act.

Without consulting anyone, I traveled to Central America, bought a small home on the beach, and lived there for the next few years. It was paradise. The weather, the beaches, the muchachas, and the laid-back lifestyle were just what I needed. I learned to play golf and to speak Spanish.

Like most people, Sicilians in particular, I had always been interested in returning to my home country, the place of my birth, so I did. It took quite an effort, but I located my Sicilian relatives. Marianna was my first cousin on my father's side and is only two weeks older than I am; well, at least back in those days she was. She introduced me to the family. To my surprise, I learned that I had a first cousin, my mother's sister's son, by the name of Salvatore Luciana, who had moved to New York with his family, and was now known as Charles "Lucky" Luciano. Marianna shared with me an unproven family rumor. "You may be his half-brother *and* his first cousin." No wonder we looked so much alike—we were closely related. I wondered how much of this was known by Lucky.

Marianna introduced me to her best friend Angila. She was even more beautiful and mature than Melissa despite her young age of only nineteen years, sixteen years my junior. We had a steamy romance and were married within a month of our meeting. We returned to live in the Central American beach house, far away from the dangerous life that came with being a mobster. It was the best time of my life. We made love standing, sitting, and lying in every room of the house, on the porch, on the beach, in the ocean and we even tried making love in our hammock but ended up flat on our backs in the sand. We took long walks along the beach in the morning, trying unsuccessfully to dodge the surf. We often slept under the stars, in our hammock or on a beach blanket. We read books, shopped in the nearby village, rode bicycles on trails in the forest, and attended Mass each Sunday. We learned to fish and sail. She taught me to cook and I taught her to speak English. In time, Angila wanted to meet my mother, who was still living in New Orleans, so in 1936 I returned to New Orleans with Angila.

This was the most time that I had spent with my mother since I left home as a teen. My mother loved Angila and vice versa. During this visit, I asked my mother about our Sicilian kinfolk, and she explained that she had been estranged from her sister for years and did not know the status of her children. She refused to tell me what had caused the rift. She denied knowing of Charlie or Lucky Luciano.

Angila wanted to see the city after spending the first few days visiting with my mother, but I felt as though I better pay Carlos a visit first, in case I was spotted by someone who knew me or mistook me for Lucky. How would I be received? One doesn't retire from the Mob, or simply vanish without permission as I had.

To my relief, Carlos was happy to see me. We shared our stories with one another, and I learned that since prohibition had ended, gambling and racketeering had become the bread and butter of the Perini family, which now reported directly to Frank Costello, who was running things for Lucky, who was in jail at the time. Simply hearing Costello's name aroused my anger, for I could never forget that he was the asshole who slipped me the mickey so that I could be butchered for Lucky's benefit. Carlos explained that there were slot machines everywhere. "Who would have thought that you could make so much money controlling labor unions?" he added. The Port of New Orleans had become the heartbeat of the New Orleans Mob. Carlos was happy to learn of my marriage and assured me that we were safe to travel about in New Orleans.

Angila loved New Orleans and America. She wanted me to sell our home in Panama and make our home in the Big Easy. I was apprehensive, because I didn't want to be drawn back into the Mob; I could live for the rest of my life on the rest of the cash that I had *earned* from being Lucky's double. But I wanted Angila to be happy, so we found a place on St. Charles and lived a quiet, peaceful life—until we received a visit from Frank Costello in 1938.

Angila answered the door and called out to me. Carlos was there to greet me. I could see past him, in the car parked curbside, that someone familiar was looking my way. It was Costello. With a knot in my stomach, I told Angila that I had some business to tend to and followed Carlos to the car. I was instructed to get in. I rode in the front seat with the driver. Carlos and Costello were behind me. It was common knowledge in gangster circles that this is not where you want to be when being taken for a ride by mobsters.

"We have an important job for you," Costello said.

My heart sank. I could not imagine being away from Angila and remembered what happened to my relationship with Melissa the last time that I went away on assignment. But I didn't feel it would be a good idea to voice my objection with Carlos sitting directly behind me so I inquired as to the plan.

"We want you to travel with Bugsy Siegel to Italy, meet with a former associate of ours you may recall: Vito Genovese. Bugsy will be accompanied by a lady friend, an

Italian countess, so you should bring your wife. It will be like a vacation. You will have a couple of weeks to enjoy Italy, so have fun. One day during your vacation, you will have to make arrangements for the women to spend the day together while the two of you meet with Vito regarding a very important matter. Bugsy has the assignment and will instruct you what to do. Your job is to be seen by Vito so that he thinks that Lucky is out of jail and running things but keep your distance. It would be bad news for you and Bugsy if Vito figures out that you aren't Lucky. The other part of your job is to watch Bugsy's back and try to keep him from doing anything too stupid. Apparently, he has this crazy idea that he is going to get a face-to-face meeting with Mussolini, and if he does, he plans to assassinate him. Keep Bugsy focused on the countess and the mission to meet with Vito. This will be the last time that we call on you. You can retire after this with another hundred grand. You have my word" said Costello.

To alleviate any concerns that I had, Costello advanced fifty grand, with the balance to be paid when the job was finished. This was too good to be true. The last thing that I said to Costello was "Hey Frank. If you get the chance; ask Lucky if he knows that we are first cousins. Our mothers are sisters."

Ben "Bugsy" Siegel and the Countess Dorothy Di Frasso

Chapter 7:
The Italian Connection

What happened in Italy that caused you to run from the mob?

Angila was a simple girl. She had nothing in common with the glamorous movie star and countess Dorothy di Frasso. The countess, as she preferred to be called, was a snob who was in awe of gangsters such as me and Ben but thought that she was too important to be in the company of commoners such as Angila. This posed a problem for Ben and I because we would have to find an excuse to leave the two of them to tend to our business, and they couldn't stand one another. We had two weeks to worry about solving the problem and intended to have fun in the meantime.

The four of us spent the better part of the first couple of days touring the Roman Colosseum, visiting the Vatican, and taking in the history of Rome. It would have been much more fun had the countess been more considerate to Angila. Late one evening, we had dinner at the Pierluigi Ristorante. Bugsy Siegel—I never called him that to his face—informed us that he and the countess had been invited to meet with Mussolini on Friday, but Angila and I were not invited. "The two of you should go on to San Vincenzo without us, and we will meet up with you in Venice." My instructions were to intercede if this situation was to occur, but I couldn't explain that in front of the girls. I waited for an opportunity to speak to Ben alone but I never had the chance, because the countess never left his side.

The next morning, Angila and I arrived by train in San Vincenzo, a beautiful small town situated on the Italian Riviera. At this point, I didn't give a damn if I wasn't following Costello's instructions to the letter. Ben was a grown man and had been in the Mob since he was a child. Not to mention that he had a reputation for being a cold-blooded killer. There was no way that I was going to argue with him. Besides, I was glad to be free of them. Angila and I had a wonderful time, sunning on the beach, dining beachside, and making love every day. We were in San Vincenzo for a week. During that time, we took the train on a day trip to Pisa to see the leaning tower and did another day trip to Florence to see David. This was the life for me; not killing people or being shot at. I made up my mind that I was finished with the Mob. I had enough money that I could start my own business somewhere, maybe there in Italy. Angila said many times that she wanted us to open a gift shop that sold perfumes.

We met up with Ben and the countess at the Hotel Londra Palace, where we stayed while in Venice. Of all the places on earth that I have visited, no other place can top Venice. It is simply the most romantic city on the planet. The people of Venice are among the friendliest and most helpful in the world. The views in every direction all over the city are breathtaking and more stimulating than my brain could process. Every narrow street was adorned with gift shops that sold shoes and women's purses, luggage, and souvenirs. "Maybe we can open a shop and live here?" Angila asked in her sweet voice. "Maybe so," I replied with sincerity. It would have been a perfect time if it had not been for the countess's relentless and progressively ruder remarks meant to insult Angila.

The Hotel Londra Palace, Venice, Italy in the 1930s

The four of us were having drinks at the Antico Martini, when Ben described his meeting with Mussolini. "He was this close and I should have killed him with my bare hands." According to Ben, German Nazis Hermann Göring and Joseph Goebbels were there also. "I didn't like those Nazi bastards." The apparent reason for the meeting was for Mussolini to purchase arms stolen from American armories, but Ben said that he wouldn't do business with the Jew-hating Nazis. Ben was fully engaged in telling this story when both the countess and Angila excused themselves. This was the first opportunity for Ben and me to talk. He quickly leaned closer to say, "We must be in Naples in three days, but we have to find a way to separate from the women." We both agreed that it would not be easy since the women despised each other.

"I've got it!" I said. "The plan is for me to be seen at a distance. The women can be in the car with me; they can be the reason that I cannot be approached." Ben thought that it was a great plan. The problem was that the women would be too close to danger for our comfort, but we chose to go with it anyway.

The women did not want to leave Venice, and neither did I, but business is business. After checking into our hotel room in Naples, Angila and I spent the next twenty-four hours in bed. We didn't even leave the room to eat, calling room service for every meal. We might never have left the room had it not been for Ben knocking persistently. "Get dressed. I need to talk to you in private, downstairs in the lounge."

He placed a briefcase on the top of the corner table. There was no one else in the lounge other than the bartender. "I've thought about it, and we can't have both of the girls with us when we do our business," he said. "Vito might recognize the countess, and that could be a problem; she's married, you know?" He went on to explain that the suitcase contained two million British pounds sterling and that we were to deliver it to Vito, as the Mob's investment in a heroin enterprise.

Ben went on to explain that the problem was that Vito felt as though he was passed over as the new Mob boss when Lucky went to jail. Vito had been Lucky's underboss, but Costello was chosen to run things for Lucky. "If he thinks that Lucky is no longer in jail, that keeps him in check, but he is going to want to approach you to find out for himself why Lucky picked Frank Costello over him as the acting boss. If Angila is with you, that will give him pause to approach you, but the countess does not need to be anywhere around. I agreed and was quite pleased with this change in plan. The meeting takes place this afternoon.

We rented a car for the occasion. Since I spoke fluent Italian, I was selected to be the driver. Ben rode in the back seat. We parked the car across from a harbor, just as Ben had been instructed. The car was positioned so that I could be seen. Ben looked at his watch, and then opened the suitcase to inspect its contents. I took the opportunity to glance at the contents as well; and it was filled with neatly stacked bills banded together, I would guess, in ten thousand pound increments. As he opened the door to exit the car, he said: "Leave the engine running, and keep the doors unlocked in case I have to make a quick getaway."

To my surprise, he left the suitcase in the car, walking down the pier empty-handed to meet Vito. I looked at Angila and asked her, "Do you trust me?"

"Of course I do," she replied.

"Then hang on, because our life is about to get really exciting."

I waited until Ben had gotten to the far end of the pier where Vito was waiting and then I pressed the accelerator to the floor and sped away. Angila screamed for an explanation.

"Look in the suitcase!"

She did. "Are we stealing money? Are you a thief?"

"This is my money. Ben told me that it was going to be used for a legitimate investment, but I just learned that he was going to use it to buy heroin, so I am backing out of the deal."

"How did you get so much money?"

"I've been saving it for years. I will explain later, but baby, these men are very dangerous, we must hide out for a little while."

She looked very skeptical but did not argue. We drove to Rome and rented a hotel room off the beaten path. Rome is a big city, which would make it more difficult to be found there than anywhere else in Italy. But knowing that Vito had become an important Mafia boss in Naples, nowhere in Italy would be safe.

. Benito Mussolini

Vito Genovese

Chapter 8:
Escape from Rome

Angila was frightened beyond my comprehension. Before meeting me, she had never left the island of Sicily. Breaking the Mafia's code of secrecy, I explained the entire story to her; she deserved that much. Of course, I omitted the part about witnessing a murder and helping to dispose of the body parts.

As a result of my impulsive act, we were now wanted by the most powerful Mafia families in America and Italy. Realizing the danger that I had placed her in, I encouraged her to leave me. "Return to your family in Sicily," I told her, but she would not leave me. She was a loyal wife.

The Mob knew all too well what I looked like, but Angila could move about the city without fear of being recognized, so she left our room from time to time to make arrangements to implement our escape plan. She exchanged some of our British money for Italian lira and Swiss francs and purchased new clothes for our disguises. Angila returned to the room after one such errand and presented a flyer that was being posted around the city. It was a picture of Lucky Luciano, with instructions to contact authorities if seen. This was evidence that the Fascist government was cooperating with the Mob in order to find me.

We changed our appearance as well as we could. We were holed up in our hotel room for two weeks, which gave me time to grow a beard. I also shaved my head completely bald, and Angila became a blonde. As an extra precaution, she purchased a pair of spectacles for me to wear.

We were now ready to make a move. Out on the street for the first time in two weeks, I stopped to take in the air. First on our agenda was to find a pay phone to make some calls. We had been afraid to do so until we were ready to relocate. Angila called her mother and explained to her that she would not hear from her for a while, but not to worry. My first call was to Carlos.

Carlos explained that Vito Genovese had convinced Mussolini to allow his drug-laden ships bound for America to use Italian ports, in return for his arranging a deal whereby the New York Mafia would sell stolen arms to the fascist for pennies on the dollar. "The deal fell apart when Ben showed up representing the American Mafia. No one figured that Mussolini would involve his Nazi ally, Hitler in the deal. Hitler's top Nazis, Goering and Goebbels were sent to attend the meeting on behalf of Germany and they refused to do business with Ben because he was a Jew. Vito was already in the port of Naples with the first shipment of drugs, waiting for Ben to arrive with the cash. Vito also refused to do business with anyone other than Italians; that's why you were there so that he would think that he was doing business with Lucky"

"Why couldn't Costello have met with Vito?" I asked.

"If Frank had shown up, Vito would have likely killed him, because with him dead, Vito would be in line to take over the Luciano family. Lucky knows that he can still run things from jail if Frank is acting boss, but Vito isn't loyal and would push Lucky to the side. The only person that Vito would not have made a move against was Lucky himself, but when you took off with the money, Ben had no choice but to explain to Vito that Lucky was in jail and you were his double. Vito vowed to return to New York and take over the Luciano family; it could mean all-out war. Either way, it's going to be really bad for you, Little Brother—have you talked to your mother?" Carlos explained.

When I answered that I had not, Carlos gave me some advice. "Johnny, you need to turn yourself in to the family."

"I can't do that, Carlos. You know that I would be a dead man."

"Cado, we go way back. You need to turn yourself in, or call your mother and tell her goodbye."

It took a moment for me to absorb his dire warning.

"I know that you are scared and I cannot protect you, but I can make it quick and easy for you, if you agree to turn yourself in to me," Carlos went on.

I hadn't considered that the Mob might take retribution out against my mother; this changed everything. Angila had been watching me and could tell that something was worrisome. "Carlos, can you assure me that nothing will happen to Mama or Angila if I turn myself into you?"

"That I can guarantee, provided you return with all of the money that you stole."

There was no other choice. I had to turn myself in to Carlos. He agreed to meet me at the airport in New York.

My next call was to my mother. "Mama, I've made a fatal mistake."

She listened to my story, but when I finished she told me, "Johnny do *not* turn yourself in. I will be safe." She then told me that she had some information that guaranteed her safety from the Mafia. "When you visited me last, you asked me if I knew that we were related to Salvatore Lucania—you call him Lucky or Charlie. I did not tell you the truth." She explained that my father had had an affair with her sister, and as a result, "You and Charlie share a father. Years later, when my sister's husband found out, he killed your father, and I fled to America with you."

This explained the uncanny resemblance between Lucky and me, but she did not tell me *what* information that she had on the Mob that kept her safe.

"These people will kill you—even your best friend, Carlos, cannot protect you. Take the money and run away to Switzerland and never return. I will be safe. I promise. Go quickly, and never look back." Those were the last words that I ever heard my mother speak.

The driver stopped the taxi curbside at the airport. In Italian, I told him to wait. "Don't drive away until I say so and keep the car running." He accepted my generous tip and agreed to do as I said. I instructed Angila to wait in the taxi while I went to the counter to buy our airline tickets.

The airport was teeming with security guards dressed in military garb. The young lady behind the counter held out her hand and with a polite smile asked for my passport. An eerie feeling that something was about to go wrong came over me, so I asked her to pardon me. "I must have left it in my case," I said.

Instead of returning directly to the taxi, I decided to survey the area. Two large men standing together near the men's bathroom, cigarettes in hand, caught my attention. They were wearing expensive suits and shoes but had the faces of brutes. Moving closer to get a better view, I could see that one had a shoulder-strapped gun underneath his jacket. It was likely the other had one also. The one with a gun had an ugly scar just below his left eye that stretched across his nose. This made me think of my own scar—the one that I woke up with after being slipped a mickey by Frank Costello. My two-week beard hid the scar from direct view, but since no hair grew on the scar itself, a side view was dangerous. Instinctively, I reached my hand to my face and stroked my short beard so as to hide the scar. Scarface noticed me noticing him. He reached into his pocket and pulled out a flyer—the one with Lucky's picture, no doubt. My heart began to pound as I walked away, trying not to call any more attention to myself. There was a large plate of glass that allowed me to see a reflection of the men following me. I stepped up the pace a bit, trying not to appear to be running away.

The men were only ten to fifteen steps away by the time I had my hand on the taxi's door handle. One of them shouted, "Halt!"

I thought that was odd. I had expected them to be Italian, but they were obviously German. I ignored the command and ordered the taxi driver to speed away.

Through the rear window I could see the two men getting into another taxi, obviously to follow us. I tossed a wad of money to the driver, I couldn't tell you how much, and instructed him to lose them no matter what it took. The driver pressed the accelerator and we zoomed through the streets of Rome, with the other taxi in hot pursuit. Our driver had impressive motoring skills, and it paid off because once we were clear of the airport, one or both of the men began shooting a gun in our direction. Angila let out a scream and our driver cursed. "Get down!" I shouted to Angila, and then I tossed another wad of cash to the driver.

The driver called our attention to some "trouble ahead." We were rapidly approaching traffic that had come to a halt. I could see behind us that there were only two cars separating us from the pursuing taxi. Seeing that we were stopped by traffic, the two gunmen jumped out of the taxi and began running toward us, guns were drawn. My first instinct was to run, but the driver shouted for us to hang on, and he turned the wheel sharply and drove the taxi onto the sidewalk, sideswiping a street vendor's cart and forcing pedestrians to scramble. The gunmen continued to pursue us on foot, running at full sprint and firing off shots, seemingly unconcerned about all of the innocent people that could have been injured or killed by stray bullets. Our driver knew this area well and quickly turned down a side street. The approaching cars dodged us as we were going the wrong way on this one-way street, but once we made a few more turns and were at a safe distance from the gunmen the driver began to inquire about our circumstances.

He assured us that the amount of money that I had thrown his way bought his loyalty and silence. He introduced himself: "I am Paolo. Let me help you," he said. "I have a friend in Milano who can give you new identities with proper papers, and help you escape into Switzerland. But we have to get you to Milano, and I cannot take you. Not to worry, I have a relative in Livorno. I can have him meet us somewhere between here and there and he will take you to Milano."

Paolo drove us to a small town near San Vincenzo where Angila and I had vacationed just a few weeks earlier. There was a scruffy young lad, no more than eighteen years of age, standing next to an old, run-down, flatbed delivery truck. The lad's name was Nicola. We thanked Paolo and said goodbye, before Angila and I crowded into the truck's cab with Nicola in the driver's seat. It was a long, rough ride to Milano.

Once there, Nicola led the way into a pizzeria, where we met Roberto. We felt it wise for everyone to keep to a first-name-only basis. After making the introductions, Nicola accepted my payment and departed. I explained to Roberto that we needed new passports so that we could pass through the border and enter into Switzerland. Roberto quoted a price, which included a room for the night. He would work all night long, but he would have what we needed by morning.

Is this when you obtained new identities?

Yes. Roberto was very talented. I was now Cicero Friddi and Angila was Maria Bartoma Friddi. We had no trouble purchasing our tickets for or boarding the train to Switzerland. Crossing the border into Switzerland was uneventful as well. We made our way to Zurich and after a good night's rest in the luxurious hotel we deposited our fortune into a Swiss bank account in our new names. It had been a huge burden, carrying around a couple of million

British pounds and knowing that almost everyone that we encountered would take our lives for that amount of money.

We spent the remainder of 1938 enjoying the splendors of Switzerland, but Angila began to grow restless. On Christmas day, she told me that she wanted to celebrate the coming of the New Year in Paris. I spent the next several days thinking about whether or not it would be safe to travel to Paris. In the end, I agreed.

Paris was beautiful that time of the year, but best of all, we felt free and safe walking the streets. We could be anyone we wanted to be there. Angila loved the city so much she made me promise that we would never leave; we agreed to open up a legitimate business and make Paris our home. Angila explained that she had always wanted to own a perfume and gift shop. This seemed like a good idea to me. We were rich and could do whatever we wanted, and if this is what she wanted, so be it.

We spent the next month searching for a place to live and a place for her store. With the help of a real estate agent, we found the perfect investment. An entire apartment building with retail stores on the first floor, located on rue Saint Lazare. There was one unoccupied retail space for the perfume and gift shop, with a nice apartment above that suited us well. Plus, it was a good investment. La Boutique de Maria opened for business in March.

Maria hired Carol Hollingsworth, a middle-aged divorcée, to manage La Boutique. Carol was British, but had been living with her husband in America. She made the move to France to start a new life following a bitter divorce from the millionaire oilman, who was determined to make her miserable if she remained in Texas.

The store was surprisingly successful, in large part due to Carol's management skills. The best decision that Carol made was to hire a twenty-four-year-old French women by the name of Collette Fountaine. Collette did not speak a word of English, but knew exactly what the young ladies of Paris wanted to purchase. Thankfully, Carol spoke both English and French.

We were settled into our apartment on the second and third floor above La Boutique de Maria. I've never been happier, before or since. We were now known as Cicero and Maria Friddi from New York, by way of Sicily. We began to make friends among other Italian and American immigrants—but our neighbors were to change our lives forever.

As the months rolled by, Maria became more and more involved with tending to the store's business, giving me time to pursue my interests. Top on my list was to do some remolding of our townhouse. Still paranoid that it was a matter of time before the Mafia would locate us, I designed and built a secret door and stairs that led to a hidden basement, which provided a means of escaping to the back alley. The project was complete by September.

The big news of the month was that Hitler's German forces invaded Poland. The subject of war and Hitler's ambitions became an all-too-frequent topic of conversation at dinner parties and other gatherings. Maria and I were not interested in politics and paid very little attention to world events. We were relieved to be in a part of the world not dominated by the Mafia, and were trying to enjoy life without a care in the world, for once.

My secret door was accessed through a pantry in the kitchen. The back wall, lined with shelves, could be opened by removing a peg, if you knew where to look for it. This gave access to stairs to the basement, which doubled as a wine cellar. I also began collecting guns, for no apparent reason other than I enjoyed buying guns. I kept the guns in the wine cellar. The wine cellar was also home to the safe, where I kept a substantial sum of cash at all times.

One Saturday afternoon, I arrived home in a new automobile that I had purchased as a surprise for Maria. The front door to the apartment was unlocked, but I did not see Maria in the living room or bedrooms. Once in the kitchen, I saw that the pantry door was open and so was the secret door at the rear of the pantry. From the top of the stairs I could make out Maria's voice coming from below: "I hope that you don't mind that I show our friends our wine cellar, dear." The two ladies with Maria were our neighbors, and since I owned the entire building they were also our tenants.

Katie was an Englishwoman who had married and divorced a Frenchman. Her friend, Ella, was an American who had recently lost a brother and a husband to untimely deaths. Soon after the second death, Ella accepted Katie's invitation to live with her in Paris.

Maria felt as though she had a lot in common with these ladies—they were all well-to-do immigrants. We became very good friends, having dinner together almost every evening. When we weren't taking turns hosting dinner, we would enjoy one of the many fine Parisian restaurants. We didn't have a care in the world.

Paris is one of the greatest cities on Earth. France was prosperous and was as big and strong as Germany, so despite the constant warnings and news reports of an aggressive Nazi war machine on the move, the dangers still seemed to be "over there."

That would come to an abrupt end on June 13, 1940.

Chapter 9:
Paris Occupied

Maria heard the doorbell ring. Katie and Ella were in a slight panic. Katie explained with a trembling voice that she had tried to call all of her friends, but no one answered, so fearing that everyone had left the city, she had instructed Ella to call the American Embassy.

Ella said that the American Embassy was surprised that I was still in the city because the entire government had evacuated and called for everyone else to do the same *yesterday*. The reason? The German Army would be in Paris in a matter of hours!

We had been so wrapped up in our lives, uninterested in what was happening on the far side of Europe that we hadn't heard the news or talked to anyone who had heard the news that the Germans were planning to attack France.

"Are you certain?" I asked.

"Of course we are certain! The city has been evacuated and we are still here. We must go in a hurry," snapped Ella.

I instructed Maria to pack the clothes while I retrieved our papers from the wine cellar. Within an hour Maria and I were in our car following Katie and Ella in their car. I asked myself: how could we have been so oblivious to current events to allow this to happen?

The highway was crowded with autos, bicycles, and people on foot; thousands of refugees jammed the road ahead of us for two hundred miles. We crept along the road, hardly any faster than the pedestrians; in fact, some pedestrians would pass us, and then we would pass them again over and over, for miles.

The sun had disappeared from the sky for an hour or so when the cars ahead of us began to blow their horns and most quickly swerved off the road into ditches and trees; some overturned. Directly ahead of us, Katie jerked her car off to the side of the road, so I followed in turn. Within seconds I saw the reason for the erratic behavior. A huge plane was bearing down on the cars, flames tracing the path of the deadly rounds from the plane to the trapped cars below. The road was all but emptied, except for a few cars that contained motionless figures.

Soon we heard the onward rush of many motors. The first to reach us was the German motorcycle troops. One politely instructed us to go back to Paris. Katie replied that we wanted to continue on to Nice, but the trooper repeated himself, this time very convincingly. Katie remarked later that he had spoken with excellent French.

We turned the cars around and drove back to Paris. Along the way, Katie and Ella wanted to stop at a roadside inn. The ladies waited in the car while I went inside, only to learn that there was no room. Upon hearing this, Katie went inside to ask the innkeeper for a glass of tea. I felt as though we were close enough to Paris and far enough from the Germans that Katie and Ella could make it safely home from here without an escort, so Maria and I drove away slowly, leaving them behind.

Upon our return to Paris, I was disgusted to see the Nazi flag flying from atop the Eifel Tower. Once we were safely in our apartment, I crawled into bed and was soon fast asleep.

The next morning I slipped on my robe, sleepily made my way to the kitchen and poured myself a cup of coffee. It was a Friday, so I assumed that Maria was likely downstairs tending to her store. After a half a cup of coffee, I began to remember the circumstances and realized that it was highly unlikely that Maria would have opened the store for business today. I figured that she must be across the hall visiting our neighbors, so I knocked on their door. No answer. I was beginning to become concerned. No one knew for certain what to expect from the German invaders or, for that matter, unconstrained civilians.

Back in our apartment, I was relieved to see Maria sitting on the sofa in our living room, coffee cup in hand. Maybe she had been in the bathroom and I hadn't noticed. My concern subsided. I sat in the chair next to her, but she asked me if I would change places with her because she wanted the sun from the window to be to her back while she read the newspaper. That was an odd request because she never read the newspaper. I became suspicious. I played along, curious as to what she was up to. She took the newspaper in hand, looking at it as if she were truly interested in reading. I don't recall exactly what she said next. It was apparent to me that she wanted to have a conversation with me, but was struggling as to what to talk about. I wasn't in the mood for conversation, and I knew that she was trying to distract me from something so I simply nodded my head or answered with a yes or no.

Suddenly something drew my attention to glance over my left shoulder and there were the ladies. Katie's arm was extended as if she was reaching for the handle of the front door, but she quickly pulled her hand back, rotated her body, and stood more erect. Ella's posture changed somewhat as well.

"Good morning. We thought we would drop by to see how you are doing this morning," Ella said.

It was obvious that they were trying to sneak out, but once caught, tried to act as though they had just walked in to visit. I knew that the door had not opened just now, which could mean only one thing. They had been in my apartment the entire time. The one place that I hadn't looked for them was in the wine cellar. It occurred to me that Maria had been working as their accomplice, serving as a decoy to distract me while they sneaked out of my apartment. I thought that I would play along for a bit, let them think that they had fooled me.

"Good morning ladies. You surprised me. I didn't hear you come in," I said and offered coffee.

"No thank you," Ella answered. "Actually, we need to tend to some things. We just stopped by to say good morning and to thank you for taking such good care of us yesterday and last night."

"I don't recall doing anything worthy of a thank-you, but you're welcome nonetheless. But why run off? You just walked in through the door, didn't you?" This was a test to see how far they would take this charade.

"Yes, but we can't stay," Katie replied nervously. "We were just checking on the two of you." Then she opened the door and told Maria and I goodbye as she scuttled out the door and across the hall to her apartment.

Ella followed close behind, waving goodbye to us. "Come to our place for lunch," she said.

The ladies were acting like two nervous high-school girls, not at all as ladies in their early sixties would be expected to behave. There was something going on that they weren't sharing with me.

Maria offered me a poached egg on toast.

"Yes, that would be nice."

I picked up the newspaper that Maria had pretended to be interested in and couldn't help but laugh out loud—the newspaper was over a week old. Maria wanted to know what had made me laugh, so I went into the kitchen where she was preparing breakfast, newspaper in one hand, my empty coffee cup in the other, and told her that I saw something in the newspaper that made me laugh. I placed the folded newspaper on the kitchen counter, with the issue date facing up. She put down the spatula and pressed her body against mine sensuously and told me to go back to the living room and relax while she served me breakfast. Then she gave me a kiss and used her hands to turn me around and gently push me out of the kitchen—but not before I noticed that she was poaching five eggs, not the usual three, for the two of us.

"Hungry?" I asked as I allowed her to push me out of the kitchen. She ignored my question and returned to her task. Then I turned back to her and said, "I would like to have a mimosa with my breakfast. I will get a bottle of champagne from the wine cellar."

"No!" she snapped with a raised voice and then, softening her tone, said, "I will get it. You have a seat and relax. I want to serve you."

"What did I do to deserve such royal treatment?" I asked and then picked up the week-old newspaper.

"Darling, I just feel especially appreciative to have you in my life, with all of the happenings going on around us."

"OK, sweetheart. I will have a seat in the living room and read today's newspaper."

I listened to her footsteps and waited until I knew she had made it to the bottom of the staircase to our secret wine cellar before rushing through the pantry and down the stairs to see what she was hiding. What I saw stunned me.

There, standing before me in my wine cellar, was a tall, fair-haired young man, wearing *my* clothes. Before I could speak he extended his hand and introduced himself as Lt. William Green, a pilot in the Royal Air Force. Maria started to explain. "He is a stranded soldier that Katie and Ella picked up last night while on the way home."

"I could not make it to the ship before we evacuated Dunkirk. Your wife and friends were kind enough to rescue me and give me sanctuary in your home. I truly appreciate it. You may have saved my life. If there is anything that I can ever do to repay you," he said. Green had been at the roadside inn where Katie and Ella stopped the night before. They had allowed him to hide in the luggage compartment of Katie's car.

Maria looked at me with pleading eyes. I didn't know what to say or do. "Maria, you better tend to breakfast before the toast burns." Her eyes lit up, remembering the toast and eggs, and rushed upstairs.

"What is the plan?" I asked the young lieutenant.

"I must find a way to the unoccupied zone, but have no specific plan," the young man replied.

Scratching my head as if it would help me think, I walked to the corner of the wine cellar where I kept my safe. I kept glancing over my shoulder to make sure that the lad couldn't observe the combination and that he wouldn't hit me over the head and take the entire contents. I looked at my handgun collection, selected my least favorite, and counted out a sum of cash that should be ample for him to pay for food, transportation, and an occasional bribe. "Here. Take this and move on. Your presence here is endangering my wife."

Maria, Katie, and Ella entered the wine cellar in time to hear my instructions. They all objected to his leaving. Katie told Mr. Green that he could stay with her until they figured things out, if he wasn't welcome in the Friddi home; each of them gave me a disapproving look. Maria began to cry. My days in the Mafia, watching men being murdered in the most gruesome manner, did not affect me like seeing Maria cry. Realizing that I was outnumbered and recalling the chances that I'd taken in the past, I agreed to allow the soldier to remain in my cellar until a plan could be developed.

The ladies gave me a big hug, and Maria added a loving kiss. Mr. Green verbalized his appreciation, and then we shared breakfast.

With Green hiding in my cellar, I felt it necessary to revitalize my old criminal networking skills. I reached out to other Italians in Paris with the goal of adding a layer of protection between the Gestapo and me, under the pretext of profiting from the scarcity of goods via the black market that was sure to develop.

Within a short time, I realized that there were no organized mobsters in Paris, at least none with connections to the Italian or American Mafia. I was likely the wealthiest and most sophisticated Italian in Paris at that time and with my experience as a mobster, I considered that I may have an opportunity to create my own Mafia family. I explained to my recruits that secrecy was always paramount to any criminal organization, and the most successful Mafia families kept their very existence secret. Back in New York, and even in New Orleans, most rank-and-file soldiers never met the Godfather or the underboss, and it was a crime to approach either of them without being instructed. In some cases, in New York, associates of the Mob didn't even know who they worked for or didn't know the head of the family's name. Their only contact was with their immediate boss.

Trying to organize a Sicilian-style or New York-style, Mafia family in France proved impossible, but I did manage to make some valuable contacts and developed a network of thieves and thugs who were willing to do my bidding for money. These associates were fascinated that I knew so much about the Mafia, and its rituals—some of which I invented—but they were soft. I explained that "The mystique of the Mafia, the perception that we are more powerful than we are, is where our power is derived."

Not all of them were soft. One of my new associates was a brute that I renamed Rocko, because it seemed to fit him better than his real name, Angelo. Rocko liked his new moniker and liked being thought of as a tough guy. He admitted that he had never killed anyone but would be willing to do so, especially if that someone were German. I had my doubts, but he was my best option to serve as my muscle. I agreed to pay Rocko a handsome sum every week, plus a percentage of the "family's" profit. To entice him even farther, he was giving the title of underboss. The title made Rocko very proud, even though it didn't mean very much. As underboss, Rocko was instructed to take orders unquestioningly and exclusively from me and to keep my identity secret from everyone, including his most trusted family or friends. Since he was to be my muscle, I provided him with a handgun, which impressed him for guns were difficult to obtain in German-occupied France.

Rocko loved his new role and followed instructions well, but he wasn't very smart and he wasn't nearly as tough as he looked; both worried me. How well would he keep a secret if the Germans were to catch him committing a crime? I had my doubts, so I was careful to keep our criminal activity to smuggling scarce commodities, which actually benefited our German occupiers.

Another Italian by the name of Drago became my consigliere. His talent was bribing Germans and other officials, making it easier for Rocko's crew to operate with impunity. He was an accountant before the invasion and knew quite a few people in important social, business, and government circles. He looked at joining the Friddi Mafia family as a thrilling adventure.

I must admit I enjoyed being the Godfather, as brief as it was. Of course, this was a pale imitation of a real crime family. However, this setup became very beneficial because the Germans soon rationed everything and even resorted to issuing food tickets. I had enough cash to buy whatever I wanted on the black market, but the prices were inflated ten- to twentyfold. Why not profit from such a markup if one can? Besides, it was free entertainment.

Rocko and Drago agreed to meet me weekly for activity reports, to settle up monetarily, and to receive new instructions from me. At one of our first high-level weekly conferences, Drago informed me that the Gestapo was methodically going house to house, block by block, street by street, searching for hidden soldiers. I knew better than to tell Drago or Rocko about the secret in my wine cellar. Information such as that would give my underlings power over me. Without giving an explanation, I instructed Rocko to hire three trusted and reliable men to watch over my house at all times. "This is the most important function of the Mafia, to protect the Godfather."

My instructions were for one man to remain close to the building's main entrance and another outside, but within a few hundred meters, and a third man was to have a getaway car ready at all times. The first soldier was instructed to stall anyone who approached the entrance to our building. He would ascertain their purpose, and if they were a danger he would discretely signal to his accomplice to create a distraction sufficient to allow the getaway driver to enter through the secret rear entrance to warn Maria and me of impending danger. No one but Maria and I knew that if this were to happen, I would have the driver take Mr. Green away, and we would remain in our home to meet the authorities.

With the hidden soldier gone, there would be no reason for Maria and me to run. Rocko and Drago assumed that I was a big fish and that if the authorities approached my building, it must be because they knew that I was a criminal kingpin.

Another week went by and we were still harboring Lt. Green. Even with the added level of security, I became more and more uneasy about putting Maria in danger. The Gestapo issued an announcement that the penalty for harboring soldiers was death. I called a meeting with the ladies and Mr. Green. We gathered around Katie's dinner table, and I made it clear to the ladies that they had to find a solution. "We cannot keep him locked away in my cellar forever."

Katie responded with good news. While she was on the subway earlier that day, she had encountered an old friend, Frederic, whom she knew from working together at the Foyer du Soldat, the French equivalent of the USO. She told us that she thought Frederic could help us, and she emphasized that she trusted him completely. She had arranged to meet with him the following afternoon.

After supper, we moved to Katie and Ella's apartment—all of us, including Green. Also present was Maggie, the maid who worked for Maria and me when she wasn't working for Katie and Ella. We sat there enjoying the last of our coffee when suddenly the doorbell rang. Maggie had a frightened look on her face when she slipped into the room and said, "The Germans are here."

I asked if they were wearing uniforms.

"No. They are civilians," Maggie answered.

"The Gestapo," said Katie. She then instructed Ella to take Green to the bedroom. "And take his coffee cup also. Try to hide him!"

I looked at Maria, angry with myself for having allowed her to be in this situation and puzzled as to why my security plan had failed. Within a few minutes, Katie instructed Maggie to allow the "gentlemen" to enter. Three plain-clothes agents entered the room and gave each one of us piercing looks and asked for our identification. Behind them was Mme Bagler, our concierge. The lead agent said that he wanted to look in the bedrooms.

Katie called out, "Ella dear, we have visitors from the police department who wish to inspect your room."

The agents walked into the room where Ella and Lt. Green were. I expected to see them return with Green under arrest, but Ella saw a picture of her brother on her dresser and remembering how Green resembled her brother came up with an idea. She instructed Green to remove his uniform, get in bed, and pretend to be sick. She quickly placed a towel on his head, just as the door was opened by the Nazi. Afterward, Ella explained that when she told the Nazis that her brother had intestinal flu, they each stepped back as if afraid of contagion. For added drama, Green moaned. When asked for his papers, Ella went to her dresser and produced her brother's old passport and driver's license. She was thankful that she had kept them all of this time. The Nazi looked at Green and then again at the photo. Green's beard made him look several years older and it was enough for him to pass as Tony, Ella's brother.

Back in the living room, the officer asked Mme Bagler for the list of tenants. He looked through it and said that he didn't see the name of the madame's brother. Katie explained that he wasn't a regular tenant and therefore he wouldn't show up on the list.

The officer looked at Mme Bagler accusingly. She explained that he wasn't on the list, because he had never asked her for a certificate of domicile.

I vouched for him also. "I'm the landlord of this building, and I live across the hall. I can verify that this is true."

The officer asked me for my papers, but told me to stay put after I said that my papers were in my apartment. He looked over the list and said, "Mr. Friddi? It says here that you are from New York. Are you an American or Italian?"

"I am both, sir. I was born in Sicily, but I became a citizen of the United States as a boy."

"Do you support Mussolini?"

"Of course! I am proud that he is returning glory to the old Roman Empire," I said, keeping a straight face.

The officer gave me a smirk, letting me know that he saw through my sarcasm, and then he sat down at the table, pulled out a writing pad and began to write something. My first thought was that he was about to write an arrest warrant, but I was relieved to see that he added Ella's brother's name to the list. We had dodged a bullet, but it was too close for my comfort.

The excuse given by the man guarding my building's entrance was that he had gone to the men's room to take a leak. He never saw the Gestapo coming. It became clear that these men would never be real professionals. This was a job to them, no more than an elevator operator. Green had to go.

The following evening, Katie told of her meeting with Frederic.

Upon hearing of Green, Frederic explained that he was part of an underground group that helped transport those who wished to join the French resistance to unoccupied France. He had explained that his organization operated a safe house where soldiers could wait until travel passes could be obtained for them. Travel pass in hand, they would take the train to "other friends who owned an estate on the frontier. From there, they travel to unoccupied France." Katie had made the point that Green didn't speak French. Frederic confirmed that could be a problem; traveling by train might not be safe for someone who didn't speak French.

Katie had offered to drive him by car to the estate. Frederic's initial reaction to that idea had been negative. He had reminded her that gasoline could not be purchased. Then he remembered that the Foyer du Soldat was still operating under the Germans. He suggested that she rejoin that organization, and then she would be provided with gasoline. As an added benefit, she would receive a Red Cross emblem for her car, enabling her to move about freely.

Katie joined the organization, obtained counterfeit travel papers for Green, courtesy of Frederic, and after stopping to deliver packages at a couple of hospitals and prisons along the way, she and Green made their way to a small town on the demarcation line where Frederic's friends awaited. She returned to tell us that her mission had been accomplished without any trouble. What a relief.

A week after Green had been crammed into Katie's luggage compartment for the final time, Maria told me that Katie received a post card from him letting her know, in code, that he was on his way to England. We were all elated, and Katie was particularly proud that she had saved her countryman. We toasted with champagne, thanks to my having a well-supplied, hidden wine cellar. "To the courageous ladies of the French Underground: May you never be so foolish again!" I said just before clinking our glasses together.

Hardly a month later, Drago and I were seated on my balcony that overlooked the rue Saint Lazare below. It was a comfortably warm summer day. From this vantage point, the German occupation wasn't so bad. Life was good once again. Drago had called the meeting and had specifically requested that Rocko not be present. He had an idea for generating revenue for the Friddi family that he wanted to share.

We hadn't finished our ceremonial small talk before business discussions when Maria called out for me with the sound of panic. It was natural for Drago to follow me to see what the emergency was; Maria had been unaware of his presence. She told Drago that she needed to see me in private right away. Drago complied by returning to his seat on the balcony. Maria led me across the hall to Katie's apartment. My reaction to what I saw inside was stated clearly: "Oh, shit!"

There on the floor was an English soldier. His pants' legs were soaked in blood and he was in obvious pain, and there was *another* Englishman in a RAF uniform kneeling beside the wounded soldier. Katie looked at me with a mix of guilt and worry. Ella said to me: "We need a doctor, but don't know who to call."

Forgetting my anger and disappointment for the moment, I answered, "I know a man who may be able to help us, and he happens to be in my apartment at this moment. One of Drago's clients in his accounting practice is a doctor that he trusts to be discreet in such matters." Soon the doctor arrived and began to treat the wounded man's leg.

I took Maria to our apartment and told her that this must stop immediately, or I would have no choice but to evict Katie and Ella. To my surprise, Maria responded defiantly: "Then you will evict me too!"

"Maria! You would leave your husband over such matters?"

She softened her voice and turned on her charm, which was substantial, and told me that although she loved me, she would rather die than turn her back on these desperate soldiers who were trapped behind enemy lines. I had never seen her so brave or so committed to anything—other than being a good wife to me. What could I say? No matter how much I pleaded, Maria was determined to help Katie and Ella to save as many young men as they could.

"Well, I suppose if I can't beat 'em, I may as well join 'em."

Soon after that, we had as many as six English soldiers at a time hiding out in our cellar. I decided to utilize my "criminal empire" to help the ladies smuggle these men to the unoccupied zone. It took all of the money that I made from our black-market enterprises and even depleted the cash that I had stashed in my safe.

My greatest fears were realized one day, beginning with the ringing sound of my doorbell—the Gestapo came calling.

The Gestapo agents took Maria and me in separate cars to Gestapo headquarters for questioning. I was ashamed of myself for not having prepared Maria for this eventuality. There was no plan in place as to what to say or what not to say, which was an amateurish mistake. Would Maria confess? There was no way for me to guess.

The German agent sitting across from me was surprisingly polite. He asked if I cared for anything to drink before we got started, and I declined. He then asked me if I was aware of criminal activity taking place in my building, and I denied any such knowledge. "We have learned that there is an underground criminal organization that is operating from within your building, and you have no idea of this?" he asked again, and once again I affirmed my previous denial.

The way he phrased this question the second time caused me to wonder which criminal organization he was referring to. Was it the small-time, petty crimes committed by the "Friddi family" or the serious crime of smuggling enemy combatants out of the country? Then it became clear that he was referring to Katie and Ella's activities but was unaware of my or Maria's involvement. He explained that he wanted Maria and me to help the Gestapo set up a sting operation to catch the ladies in the act of smuggling soldiers. I acted as if I were appalled that anyone would commit such a crime and angry that it was happening in my building. "Of course I will cooperate!" I could only hope that Maria was giving the same answer. If so, we may have dodged another bullet, because I am sure that Katie and Ella would fall on a sword to protect us.

Another plain-clothes German agent entered the room. He looked familiar. I studied his face, wondering where I had seen him before. Then I recognized the scar that began under his left eye and stretched across his nose. It was Scarface from the airport in Rome! I stared for too long. He saw that I recognized him and began to study me. I had changed my appearance a bit more since Rome. When he last saw me, I was wearing a beard and glasses and sporting a shaved head. I still had my beard but no longer wore the glasses, and the hair on my head had grown back. Maybe he didn't recognize me—after all, our last encounter was nearly a year ago. Wait a minute! I began to wonder how he had recognized me in Rome. After all, he should have been looking for someone who looked like Lucky, and I had disguised my looks quite well.

Scarface reached over and grabbed my chin and turned my face so that he could see my L-shaped-scar reminder of my days as a member of the Masseria-Luciano family. He then whispered something into the polite agent's ear, who suddenly rose from his chair and left the interrogation room. He returned with two members of the dreaded SS. Scarface spoke: "This man, Charles Lucky Luciano, is an important man in whom the führer himself has an interest."

"Wait! There is a mistake. I am not Luciano. I've been mistaken for him before, but Luciano is in jail in America," I exclaimed.

"Nice try. We know that is American propaganda. You escaped with a great deal of money that belonged to the Third Reich."

Oh, shit. How the hell did that happen? I wondered. How could the money that I stole from Ben belong to the German government? The Germans would not do business with Jews, so how could Ben Siegel, a Jew, gain possession of money that belonged to Nazi Germany?

Scarface instructed the polite agent to arrest me. "He will be traveling to Berlin with me."

The Germans march on Paris.

Chapter 10:
Working for Hitler

The next several weeks were spent rotting away in a Gestapo jail in Paris. The worst part about it was that I wasn't able to hear from or about Maria. Had they arrested her also? Would I ever see her again? Would I even have the opportunity to tell her goodbye and that I loved her one last time?

The jail cell doors were flung open. Two uniformed SS men handcuffed my hands and my feet and escorted me to the street, where I was placed in the back of a jeep. There were three armed guards in the jeep with me, and two other jeeps with armed guards, one in front of us and one behind us, which accompanied us all the way to Berlin. It was a long and uncomfortable trip. I was taken to a holding cell and left there for three days before I had any visitors.

Scarface returned, escorted by a couple of members of the SS. They relocated me to a large government administrative building adorned with Nazi flags. We were instructed by a secretary to wait. Soon the secretary's phone rang. After she answered she looked at Scarface and said, "The führer will see you now."

Behind the large oak desk was a timid-looking man with glasses. He looked as if he were an accountant. He introduced himself as Heimlich Himmler, the chief of the SS, and then he introduced Joseph Goebbels, chief of the propaganda ministry. Himmler congratulated Scarface on catching a big fish and assured him that he would receive recognition. Then he looked at me and said, "Welcome to Berlin, Herr Luciano. We are mystified to have such an important American gangster in our presence."

At this point, I wasn't certain if it were in my best interest to allow them to think that I was Luciano or not, so I decided to keep my options open for the time being. I answered in the manner that I thought Luciano would answer. "The feeling is mutual, Herr Himmler."

Himmler smiled and asked, "Did you enjoy spending the führer's money?"

"If I had known the money belonged to anyone other than the Mob, I wouldn't have taken it."

"What did you do with the money?" he asked.

I explained that I had purchased real estate in France and spent a lot of the money on various things, but most of it had been spread among various banks in Switzerland, England, and Canada. I felt that it was important to be truthful about this, for Maria's sake.

"Did you have any trouble spending it? No problems with depositing the money in any of those banks?'

"No, none whatsoever. If we could just forget this whole matter, I will round up what's left of the money, sell the real estate, and I may be able to return the full amount that I took. I made some good investments."

Himmler, still smiling, opened a briefcase atop his desk and said, "That's OK. You did us a favor." He then removed a stack of British sterling pounds from the brief and placed it in front of me. "There are twenty thousand pounds. Take it. It's yours. I want you to paint the town with your wife this coming New Year's Eve."

"What? Is this some sort of joke?" I asked.

"We don't joke about such matters, Herr Luciano. We have a proposition for you. The money that you stole is counterfeit—made right here in Berlin." He paused to see my reaction. I was stunned, but I didn't show it. "We realize that you are in a predicament. You can't return to America—the Mob will kill you. You cannot return to Italy, because if the Mob doesn't kill you, Mussolini will. If you try to escape to England, we will kill your wife first and then you."

"What do you want me to do?"

"I think that you are going to like this assignment." Himmler explained that his plan was to devalue the British currency by flooding the market with counterfeit money. "Your job is to spend like there is no tomorrow, with emphasis on circulating the money internationally."

Goebbels instructed me to get as much of the money into the hands of the Mob as possible. "Use it to buy heroin from your old pal, Vito Genovese, and sell the poison to the American Mob in return for American dollars, which you will deposit into a German bank account that we designate."

Himmler suggested that I travel to Argentina and make some real estate investments there and elsewhere. "In case you get any bright ideas about trying to slip away, know that you will be under strict surveillance at all times. Your wife's passport has been collected. She will not be allowed to travel abroad. If you make any attempts to escape, you will receive a life sentence of hard labor, and she will receive punishment more severe than you can imagine. Those are your options: live like a king, or die a slow and miserable death."

"You aren't giving me a difficult choice," I replied. There was no point in mentioning the unlikelihood that Vito Genovese would rather do business with me than to kill me, and ditto for the American mobsters.

"Yes, but we do not want an answer from you until after you've seen something that we have in store for you tomorrow," Himmler said.

Instead of returning to jail, I spent the evening as Himmler's house guest. He was hosting a dinner party for none other than the führer himself Adolf Hitler. This was an incredible turn of events. Earlier in the day, I was in a jail cell, thinking that I was destined to have a noose around my neck, and now I was being treated as a dignitary.

Himmler introduced Hitler to me. Hitler looked me in the eye and said something in German, but I wasn't sure if it was intended for me or Himmler. He did not extend his hand to shake, and neither did I. Himmler and Hitler had a short conversation in German, obviously about me, because I heard the name Luciano a couple of times, then Hitler walked away to talk with others at the party.

Himmler looked at me and said, "Lucky for you that the führer agrees that you might be useful to the Third Reich."

"Herr Himmler, may I ask a question?"

UnLucky Double

"Of course, Herr Luciano."

"How much money are we talking about? How much do I get to spend?"

"As much as you can before the world realizes that it is counterfeit money. More is better, but just so that you know, we've printed nearly thirty million pounds sterling and can print more any time that we want."

"There is nothing that you can show me that can change my mind. I accept the offer."

"I am certain that what you see tomorrow will not change your mind, but will give you something to remember in case you ever need reassurance that you made the right decision."

The next morning I was driven by Himmler to a medical research facility in Dachau, where I was introduced to Dr. Sigmund Rascher.

"Welcome to the world's premier medical research program. Come this way, gentlemen." We were led to a room where we were seated to view through a large pane of glass some of the doctor's research. Another man wearing a lab coat that matched Dr. Rascher's entered the room. Rascher made the introduction. "This is Professor Dr. August Hirt of the Strasbourg Anatomical Institute, which has provided the grant for the research into the effect of high altitude on flyers."

Professor Hirt, as he preferred to be known, said, "We believe this valuable research will save the lives of many Luftwaffe pilots."

We were informed that an experiment was about to begin. We turned our attention to the room on the other side of the glass. Rascher explained that we were looking at a decompression chamber. A naked man, escorted by two men in lab coats, was placed in the chamber, which had a glass door enabling us to see his entire body inside the tiny space. The machine began to make a rumbling noise, and an indicator dial at the top of the chamber began to move. The naked man began to wince, obviously in pain. The dial moved some more. Himmler whispered in my ear, "Do not look away." The tortured man began convulsing, his hands and head taking turns banging on the glass door. Then suddenly, his leg burst. It was awful, and I couldn't help turning away.

Himmler spoke in a commanding tone this time. "Keep watching." The poor soul in the chamber began pulling his hair in an effort to relieve the pressure. The dial turned more, and then he started tearing at his face, then hitting his head with all his might against the chamber, trying anything to stop the suffering. The dial turned more, and suddenly the man exploded into a bloody mess. I lost it. I threw up my breakfast right there on the spot.

Himmler leaned over and said, "You needed to see what will happen to your wife, should you ever disappoint me."

"You made your point. I get it. You had me with the money."

UnLucky Double

The image of the man exploding in front of me kept playing over and over in my mind, no matter how hard I tried to think of something else. Himmler seemed unaffected. He laughed at his own jokes all the way back to Berlin. I had heard the Germans were sick bastards, but how could anyone even imagine this cruelty?

The trip home to Paris was much more enjoyable than the bumpy car ride to Berlin. I was flown with Scarface on a luxury plane owned by the Luftwaffe. Scarface's name was Hans Fischer, and he was assigned the responsibility to supervise me. Himmler had instructed him that wherever I went, he would go.

Our first stop was to get Maria out of jail. We were so happy to see one another. We hugged so tightly that I was afraid that I was going to hurt her. Scarface dropped us off at our apartment, and I recall how odd it was that he told Maria politely how pleased he was to have made her acquaintance. Are these fucking people insane? He shot at us, threw us in jail, and then tells us that he is pleased to make our acquaintance. Geez.

Maria and I made love that night as never before—over and over, all night long. The next morning we gave one another a report. She went first and explained that Katie and Ella had been arrested and charged with high treason.

"There is nothing that we can do for them, I explained."

Now it was my turn to give her my report. I contemplated whether or not to tell her everything, including the scene at the Nazi medical research facility. I made the decision to tell her everything, so that she would know what we were facing in the event we tried something stupid, like trying to rescue another English soldier. She trembled in my arms and wailed like a baby after I told her what I had seen. We cursed the Germans, the Nazis, and most of all, we cursed Hitler. We were unaware of the listening devices that the SS had installed in every room in our apartment. In the end, the Nazi spies heard us agree that we had no choice but to do our very best to serve our German masters well.

Himmler instructed me to get to work right away upon my return to Paris. The Germans set up a special number for me to use so that I could call anyone in the world without them knowing my whereabouts. I called my mother's number, but it had been disconnected. Carlos's number was next. He was very surprised to hear from me, but after we exchanged pleasant greetings, he told me the bad news. My mother was dead. He couldn't say who did it, but it was a hit in retribution for my taking the Mob's money. My heart sank. She had said that she had something on the Mob that would keep her alive. Now I realized that she was just protecting her little boy. Carlos gave me a few minutes to gather myself following that news, and then we began to talk business.

"VG is trying to return to New York if he can make his legal troubles go away. If that happens, there may be a war. He is determined to replace the prime minister as the boss, and that means war."

VG was code for Vito Genovese and the prime minister was code for Frank Costello. As Carlos was telling me this, it occurred to me that the Nazis were likely listening in on this conversation, and it was beneficial for them to think that I was Lucky, so I replied, "It may be time for VG to know that I am not in jail but am in full control of the family once again. I have a plan."

The phone went silent. Carlos wasn't sure if I was talking in code or if I had lost my mind. "OK, let's hear it." It was highly unusual for mobsters to talk business on the telephone, but we didn't have much choice. I had to be conscious of the fact that someone on the American side might be listening in on our conversation as well.

"First, I need to know if all will be forgiven if I repay my debt with interest. If that is possible, tell me how much it will take. I am willing and able to pay my debts, whatever the amount."

"I will see what I can find out. Give me a few days," Carlos replied.

The news of my mother's death was difficult to handle. Losing your mother is bad enough, but to know that you are responsible for her death is worse. My hatred for the Mafia festered—Frank Costello, Vito Genovese, and Ben Siegel especially. I had a burning desire for revenge, but then I saw the image of the exploding man and thought of Maria. I had to control my desire for revenge in order to keep her safe; unless I could find a way to get revenge that benefited the Nazis.

The wheels were in motion with the Mob; next on the agenda was to plan the biggest and most extravagant New Year's Eve party in the history of Paris. For this, I needed Drago.

Professor August Hirt

Dr. Sigmund Rascher

Chapter 11:
Argentina

By December 31, 1941, most Parisians had gotten more or less used to German occupation, and some even accepted it as the new normal—the way it was, and was likely always going to be. A happy populace would benefit the Germans, especially the Propaganda Ministry. For this reason, Goebbels became personally involved with planning the event. Maria and I were official hosts, but the Nazis were determined to make sure the party was a success. My job, which I delegated to Drago, was to invite as many influential Parisians as possible.

Maria contacted Collette, the cute young girl who had worked for her in La Boutique Maria before the invasion, and instructed her to make a list of as many young men and women as she knew, and they would be invited to this spectacular gala.

But unfortunately, all but a few Parisians boycotted the gala. Despite the enormous amount of money spent on promoting the event, the decorations, and the entertainment, it was a flop. Germans occupiers outnumbered the Parisian guests by ten to one, at least. The worst part about it was that Maria and I were now looked upon as Nazi collaborators. Little did they know how much we despised the Nazis, but there was our name, printed on invitations that were mailed to everyone who was anyone.

More than a few Nazis made a point of letting me know that they were disappointed at my inability to draw a crowd of Parisian socialites. What did they expect? First of all, I was an unknown, Italian American immigrant, married to a simple Sicilian girl, in a town occupied by the most hated people on Earth.

Even Collette failed to show. She gave Maria a weak excuse, too weak to even recall. Drago's friends didn't show either. The Parisian women that attended the party were labeled as whores and became shunned by the civilian population; so much for Maria and I being the toast of the town.

Once I recovered from my hangover, it was time to get back to work. Carlos was successful in getting Vito and the real Lucky to agree to have a meeting in which Albert Anastasia would be there on behalf of Lucky. I emphasized to Carlos, "Don't send any Jews this time or the deal may fall apart once again."

Himmler ordered Hans to protect me at all costs, and a call was made to Mussolini. The Italian Army had a small squadron at the airport to greet me and my Nazi protectors. There must have been two dozen agents with their eyes on me at all times. The meeting was held in Naples, at a small, discreet café in the heart of town. Vito, Albert, and I did not exchange small talk; we were all business.

"You caused a great deal of trouble, taking off with that money like that," Vito began.

"That is why I am here; to rectify the situation."

"I should kill you right here," he replied.

"That would not be a good idea."

Albert Anastasia spoke up. "Gentlemen. We are here today to determine the proper compensation owed to the aggrieved parties. If we can satisfy the financial concerns, then all personal problems will go away. Agreed?"

"Agreed," Vito nodded.

I looked Vito in the eye and asked: "Give me a number. What is it going to take to make things right with you?" It was easy for me to be brave; I had the full support of the German and Italian Armies watching out for my safety.

"Half a million dollars, American," Vito said without hesitation.

That was a surprisingly low number. "How did you come up with that figure?"

"That's my number."

"OK, but would you accept twice that amount in British sterling pounds?"

Vito laughed as if it were the dumbest question that he had ever heard and said, "Fuck yes."

Albert Anastasia laughed also and said, "I can't wait to do business with you. I was going ask for half a mill also, but I want the same thing that Vito gets."

I shook my head and agreed, but then said, "I don't get it. I stole two million from you. What gives?"

Vito answered first. "You didn't steal anything from me, except time. I had to sit on that shipment until Lucky could send someone with better sense than Ben to deliver the money."

"Same here," Albert added. "That was Mussolini's money. Half was to go to Vito to pay for the goods that he was to deliver to America, and the other half was to go to New York to buy guns that would return on Vito's empty cargo ship. We were out an opportunity, but we didn't lose any direct cash."

"Then who killed my mother?"

The two men froze. The silence lasted for several seconds, and then they both responded at the same time, stating that they didn't know anything about that. I leaned back in my chair and thought for a second, asking myself: If not them, then who did it? Who was motivated to take revenge on me by killing my mother?

"I have a proposition for the two of you. I will give you one million British pounds each, today, to compensate for your past troubles. I will give you another one million British pounds each to do the same deal that was planned before. Vito, you deliver your product to my friends in New York, and in return, you bring back to this port two million pounds worth of high-quality armaments, to be turned over to Mussolini's government."

"You've got this all worked out?" Vito asked.

"Yes."

"How the fuck did you do that?"

"Yeah, how the fuck did you get to be friends with Mussolini, especially after you stole his money before?" Albert asked.

I waved over to Hans as was planned and said, "Don't worry about it."

Two Italian soldiers and two German SS walked over to the table. Two suitcases were placed on the table, one in front of Vito and one in front of Albert. Albert and Vito looked around. They could easily see half a dozen or more men who were obviously watching us, as my protectors. Some were wearing Italian military uniforms and some were wearing plain clothes, but all displayed rifles in plain sight. The message was clear: I had two armies backing me up.

"Your money is inside. You can count it if you like. Two million British pounds are in each case. If this goes well, you will have a repeat customer. If it doesn't go well, then Vito, you may need to find a base in which to operate outside of Italy."

Vito was flabbergasted. "I don't know who you fucked or sucked to get this kind of power. I've been supplying Mussolini's son-in-law with cocaine for years, and I don't have this kind of clout."

With my hand offering a shake, I said: "Then can we agree that the Luciano family is at peace with the Genovese family? And, Siegel, are we all good?"

"As far as New York is concerned, we are all family once again. Forget about Bugsy. He is in California, and won't be involved to screw anything else up among us again," Albert replied.

Vito agreed and we all shook on it. A handshake with a Mafia Godfather is a contract that one can count on more than anything written.

There was a time when I considered the Italian Mafia as the most dangerous criminal organization in the world, but they were Girl Scouts compared to the swastika-wearing bastards that had me by the balls. We agreed that it would take time, maybe a year, for the parties to provide the amount of product that this much money could buy, but my parting statement was intended to foster more activity, quicker: "If you know of any other investments that need funding, please give me the first opportunity. Nothing is too big."

In a final show of pageantry, several armed men in plain clothes hurried from across the street toward us the moment we stood. Vito and Albert looked at me accusingly, and Albert asked, "What's this?"

"Nothing to worry about. These men are simply here to protect me," I replied as I walked away with the armed men surrounding me. They opened my car door for me and I slid inside. Hans was waiting for me in the back of the limousine, which was parked across the street where he could see and hear my performance. Still in his lap was the headset that had allowed him to listen to our conversation. He very pleased with my performance.

"Halt at the next phone booth, I must make a telephone call at once," he instructed the driver. As per his instructions, he phoned Himmler to provide him with a report and to receive our next instructions. Hans got back in the car and looked at me and said, "Berlin, here we come."

Please clarify for the court, you returned to Berlin in June of 1941?

"Yes. Six months had passed since the Mafia peace accord was struck in Naples. War fever had a firm grip on the whole of Germany, and in order for Hans the Scarface to keep a watchful eye over me, I had to operate from Berlin. He called early one morning and instructed me to be ready to be picked up by nine. "Dress formally," he told me.

The meeting was held in a conference room at SS headquarters. There were a dozen participants sitting around the long table, counting me. Himmler was standing in front with another member of the SS, whom I didn't recognize. His name was never mentioned, so I assume that everyone there—other than me—knew his name; I was the only non-German in the room. Himmler began by stressing the importance of keeping the existence of this high-level meeting top secret.

"The very existence of the organization must not be revealed to anyone outside of the highest levels of the SS, all of whom are in this room at this very moment." Himmler then addressed me: "Herr Luciano, you are here because you can fill a necessary role in a very important operation that is designed to insure the permanency of the Reich. You are hereby ordered to give your loyalty to this group and swear an oath of silence on the life of your pretty wife."

The man standing next to Himmler motioned for me to join him at the front of the room. He placed a Bible in the podium and required me to repeat the solemn vow with one hand raised and the other on the Bible. It seemed at first completely unnecessary, for the remainder of the meeting was in German, which I knew very little, until Himmler summarized the meeting in English for my benefit.

"There is no doubt that Germany will win the war, but our job at the SS is to see that the Reich is prepared for any and all contingencies for its survival. One such contingency that all nations must prepare for is occupation by a foreign enemy, requiring the temporary relocation of government. The men inside this room are charged with this mission. You will help them by accompanying them to Argentina, where you will open a bank account in your name, make a substantial deposit of British pounds, and then you will purchase properties as directed. You will then be instructed to convey your properties to people and corporations that benefit our mission. As I've said, the very existence of this organization could be detrimental to the morale of the German Army and populace. You would be well advised to remember our conversation at Dachau. Your file states that you are fluent in English, Italian, and Sicilian. Can you understand Spanish?"

Himmler and the rest of the group were pleased to learn that I am fluent in Spanish. "Telephone your wife to let her know that you may not communicate with her for the next several months. There will be no international phone calls made by anyone in this group while in Argentina."

The sense of urgency and secrecy led me to believe that Himmler thought Germany's defeat was inevitable. Maria and I were sad to know that we would not see one another or even talk on the telephone for several months. We had seen one another for one weekend each month for the past six months. It made no sense to us that the SS required her to remain in Paris while I was assigned to Berlin, but the Germans always have a reason for everything.

Hans sat next to me on the plane to Rio de Janeiro. He explained that I was to play the role of a wealthy American businessman who was searching for real estate investment opportunities in Argentina.

"You have no interest in politics and you have never been to Germany. Your German escorts are your servants and bodyguards. You will hire some locals to serve these roles as well, so that you don't draw attention to the fact that you only have German staff."

I asked Hans why only six from the group of twelve were joining us on this trip. He explained, "This operation is bigger than Argentina. There must be escape routes, safe houses, transportation systems in place." I asked him if he thought that German officials would have to use these escape routes. "No, but every government has contingency plans for such things. America is at peace, but the president of the United States has a bomb shelter under the White House."

He made a good point, but the amount of resources that Germany expended in Argentina during a time of war said something different. Over the course of a year that I spent in Argentina, we purchased hundreds of homes, ranches, and even entire apartment buildings. More telling was the fact that there were already a hundred or so Germans, presumably Nazis, in Argentina developing a network. As far as I could see, we never met with any Argentine government officials. This was a silent invasion.

The most notable property that I purchased was the Hacienda San Ramón. Prior to the purchase, several high-ranking Nazis, mostly members of the SS, flew in to tour the Hacienda before the purchase. Strangely, one of them was Professor Hirt, one of the quack research doctors from Dachau. A group of us that included, among others, Hirt, an architect, an engineer, and a local contractor, toured the place. I served as interpreter, for the contractor spoke only Spanish. There were a lot of questions pertaining to electrical requirements and backup generators. Immediately after touring the Hacienda, we were taken by mule to a site high in the Andes Mountains. It was freezing cold even in July. Once again, Hirt and the engineers seemed to be mostly concerned with the ability to maintain electrical power at all times. The contactor's answer each time was that it would be very expensive, but enough generators and backup generators could guarantee permanent power at all times even way up here in the Andes. We purchased the Hacienda and the remote property in the Andes. An Argentine lawyer created a trust for which I was instructed to convey these and other properties. The German architect presented the contractor with plans for building and renovating the Hacienda and building a compound in the Andes.

A lot changed during the year that we were in Argentina, but nothing was more significant than America entering the war. I was thrilled that Hans and I were ordered to return to Berlin. I missed Maria. While on the flight home, I asked Hans why Dr. Hirt would be interested or involved in building a compound way up in the Andes Mountains, and his reply was startling: "Something to do with freezing experiments. That's all that I know."

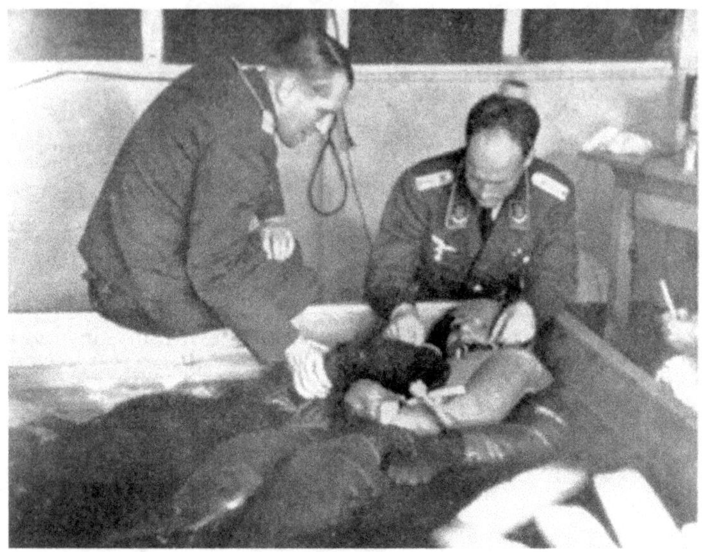

Rascher and Hirt submerging a prisoner in ice
during a "freezing experiment"

Lidice Memorial, Czech Republic

Chapter 12:
Deep Sleep

It was May 1942 when the wheels of the plane stopped and the door opened for us. Waiting for us was an official German SS staff car, bearing two Nazi flags, one above each headlight. One of the soldiers opened the car door so that we could climb inside. Hans and I were surprised and concerned that the highest-ranking SS officer, Heinrich Himmler himself, was there to meet us at the airport. Hans looked especially worried. Himmler was agitated. With restrained anger in his voice he asked me, "Have you followed my strict orders to have no communications with anyone outside of Argentina?"

"Yes of course," I replied. The ramifications of not following orders were clear to me and I would not do anything that could jeopardize Maria's safety.

"Herr Himmler, may I respectfully ask what this is about?" asked Hans.

Himmler answered in German, but I could understand only a few words, including *"der führer."*

"Did you have any communications with your gangster friends in New York while we were in Argentina?" Hans asked me.

"No! I've made no calls, not even to my wife. What am I being accused of?"

Hans told me that *der führer* himself wanted to answer that question. Hans didn't have to explain how serious the charges were for Hitler to address them personally during a war whose outcome it seemed would determine the very existence of civilization.

With Himmler leading the way, we walked past all checkpoints straight to the office where Hitler and the minister of propaganda, Joseph Goebbels, were waiting for our arrival. Hitler was in a foul mood and began by shouting questions at me in German. Hans interpreted for us: "The führer wants to know how and why you were able to convince longshoremen in the United States to spy against the Third Reich." Himmler handed a report to me, which had been transcribed into English for my benefit.

The report claimed that Lucky Luciano had ordered the members of the longshoremen's union to cooperate with the American police. As a result, a German American spy ring had been uncovered and several attempts of sabotage had been foiled. It was time to reveal my true identity.

"I am not Lucky Luciano. My name is Giovani Cado. Luciano and I look virtually the same as twins, in part because we are half-brothers—sons of the same father."

Himmler and Hans told Hitler that my story must be true, because I had been of valuable service to the Third Reich, and there were no records of any foreign calls made by me in Argentina. Hitler calmed down and after reflecting on the conversation said, "This is a plausible explanation. Keep him Berlin. I may have more use for him."

UnLucky Double

Maria was on the next train to Berlin. Our reunion was divine. Each time we separated, we seemed closer with each reunion. She was to return to Paris after three days, but I went over Hans and straight to Himmler to request that she stay with me in Berlin, and he agreed.

The English were onto the German's counterfeit scheme, which resulted in their recalling all notes to be replaced with an entirely new design. The German response was to do the same thing to the Americans. The counterfeit printing press went into action, and I was charged with devising a plan to pump the fake American money into the international economy.

Hans was anxious for me to unload the two million American dollars onto the market somehow, but it was hard to operate from Berlin. Cities were being bombed on a regular basis, knocking out telephone service. The Allies were intercepting calls from Germany.

To make matters more difficult, Vito Genovese switched sides after America joined the war and had returned to New York. Mussolini cut off all Italian ports for his use. The New York Mob never delivered the weapons either. I had to come up with another plan to distribute the counterfeit money into the world's economy.

Weeks went by without my having devised an acceptable plan, and Himmler was growing impatient with me.

Hans was ordered to drive me to the Czech town of Lidice to witness another gruesome Nazi atrocity on the morning of June 10, 1942. In retaliation for the assassination of a German general, the town was surrounded by German troops who rounded up all of the men and boys over the age of fifteen, and made the women and children watch while they were executed. Then the Nazis systematically burned building after building. Next, construction crews cleared all of the debris, roads, monuments, and every last remnant of the town, so that there was no evidence that it had ever existed. Finally, the women and children were hauled away to labor camps.

"Why did Himmler want me to see this?" I asked Hans.

"He wants to motivate you. He thinks that you are stalling on your assignment out of loyalty to America. He wants you to know how ruthless he can be to enemies."

"Tell him that I got it the first time."

Himmler's plan worked. I devised a plan the very next day. It involved my old pals, Drago and Rocko. Hans would have to get permission to allow them to travel overseas with the money. My request was granted.

Maria and I returned to our apartment in Paris and put in a call to Drago and Rocko to tell them that I had a lucrative job for them. A meeting was held a day later, on my balcony overlooking the rue. The first hour or so was spent on small talk, as was our tradition, but then it was time to get down to business. Maria brought two small suitcases on cue, handing one to each of my friends. Rocko and Drago opened the cases and stared at a million dollars each. Rocko's jaw dropped. Drago was also speechless.

"Each suitcase has the proper travel documents for both of you to travel to a little country in Central America called Panama. You are to go there and deposit half of this money in an account in my name, and you keep the rest. If you do exactly as I've instructed, we will do this again, and again, with each amount becoming larger."

Drago, being the accountant, wanted to know more details, so I explained that all the arrangements had been made for them to be flown to Spain, then Malta, then South America, and then to Panama. They were to depart right away.

Maria and I spent the next several days in Paris. It was good to see Carol and Collette, the only other people in France other than the Nazis who would talk to us. Other neighbors gave us dirty looks as we walked by. One teenage boy followed us home, and once we were inside our apartment, a brick was thrown through our window. The brick had a swastika scratched on it to let us know the reason for the attack. We returned to Berlin the following day.

The war created enough distraction that I was all but forgotten, for the time being. Hans stopped following me around and our meetings became more and more infrequent. The idea of escaping crossed my mind. Maria and I went for a walk through the city and to a park. We double-backed enough times to be certain that no one was following us. Once completely comfortable that we were able to speak freely, I told her that I thought that Germany was going to lose the war. "If that happens, we will be tried as traitors to our country. If given the chance to escape, we need to take it. But where would we escape to? We can't go back to America or Sicily."

"Panama. We still own a home there, on the beach; and I have a substantial amount of money in a bank there."

Maria began to tremble. She was terrified of the Nazis, and rightfully so. She wanted to know how we could escape this terrible place.

"The SS provided me with fake identities and traveling papers for Drago and Rocko to take counterfeit money to Panama. I am going to try the same thing, but this time I am going to see if I can get travel papers for their wives as well, but you and I will go in place of Drago and his wife. Did you notice how little we were watched by Hans and the SS this last time that we were in Paris? I think that either we've gained their trust, or they are so busy with higher priorities that we aren't as big of a concern as we once were."

Heinrich Himmler and Adolf Hitler

"What will happen to us if we are caught?"

"That is too horrible to think about. We must not try unless we have a high probability of success."

The wheels were put into motion right away. Within days Hans delivered four million counterfeit dollars and travel papers for two married couples. A meeting was held to explain the plan to Rocko and Drago. Once again, from our Paris apartment balcony overlooking the rue, we started with small talk, but I wanted Maria to participate in the conversation this time.

Drago described their previous journey to Panama in great detail. "It was virtually event free. The Germans assisted us to the demarcation line and from there it was no problem making our way to Spain."

It was now time for me to explain my plan. "I have something to ask of you, Drago. It could be dangerous."

"Anything for my Don," he said with a smile.

Realizing that the Nazis had likely planted listening devices in my apartment, I whispered the plan in his ear.

After hearing my plan Rocko and Drago left our apartment with their suitcases filled with fake money and traveling papers. That evening at precisely ten o'clock, Maria and I opened the pantry and walked down the stairs to my hidden wine cellar. On the far side was a section of the wall that opened inward with a pull. From the outside, there was no evidence that this part of the wall opened as a door. There Drago and his wife were, right on cue. They entered through the secret door. Drago's wife presented Maria with a wig, and Drago presented me with an extra pair of eye glasses and his top hat and overcoat. We traded house keys, and before Maria and I said goodbye for the final time to our most loyal friends, we told them our real names.

We walked to Drago's house, which was no more than ten blocks away, entered their house and waited for Rocko and his wife to appear the next morning. They were right on schedule. Maria was wearing the wig and I was wearing the items given to me by Drago. We had no trouble boarding the train that took us to a frontier town on the demarcation line. There had been no sign of Hans.

Our plan seemed to have worked. We disembarked from the train with the intention of boarding another that would carry us to unoccupied France, but there was Scarface! We had gone too far to get caught, so I leaped into action by rushing Scarface and tackling him. "Run, Maria! Help me, Rocko."

Rocko sprang into action too. He grabbed Maria, wrapping both arms around her so that she could not run away. Within seconds three other SS men were on the scene, pulling me off of Hans.

"Rocko?"

"I'm sorry, Cicero. I'm an agent for the Gestapo."

My heart sank. The plan was so perfect. We would have made it, had it not been for that treacherous Rocko. Now what was in store for us? I begged Hans to forgive us, to give me another chance. I promised that if he would forget this whole thing, that I would do spectacular things for the SS. If nothing else, please let Maria go. I begged and begged.

I was detained at Gestapo headquarters in Paris until I could be transported back to Germany. Once again, Maria and I were separated. My memories of what I saw at Dachau and Himmler's words whispered in my ear played over and over in my head. Suicide would be much better, if only I could find the opportunity.

Gestapo agents rode with me on the train back to Germany. Just as I had feared, I was taken straight to the medical research facility in Dachau. Bound in a straitjacket, I waited in a padded cell. Rascher and Hirt appeared with two orderlies. I'm not proud to say that I was more frightened than I had ever been. The image of that man tearing at his face, ripping out his hair and banging his head on the glass, trying anything to stop the pain before he burst right open, was worse when I realized that was likely going to me my fate, but even worse, Maria's fate. I cried like a scared little boy and screamed, "Please, *please!* Don't do it. I will do anything. I'm begging you!"

Rasher instructed Hirt to inject me with a sedative. I jerked as much as I could, trying to avoid the needle, but it was useless. He injected something in my neck and soon I felt very relaxed. I stopped screaming and my eyelids grew heavy.

Hirt leaned down to talk. "There is no reason to fear. You are not going to be hurt or killed. The experiment that we are going to perform on you is for the good of science, for mankind, and the Third Reich."

Then, everything went black.

Part Two

Escape from the Nazis

2046 AD

"All rise!"

The crowded courtroom followed the bailiff's instructions. Three judges entered the room and took their places. Johnny Cado couldn't help but think how strange it was that all three judges were women—and one of them was black and one Hispanic. In his time, women couldn't even vote, and blacks couldn't drink from the same water fountain as whites. He could only imagine what Adolf Hitler would think about this.

The prosecutor was a bald, German-looking white man who had done most of the talking thus far. His attorney, the court-appointed public defender, was a young black man who had yet to object to a single thing.

The media and other observers returned to their places in the pews where they had sat before the recess. The audience included high-ranking officials with Homeland Security and the National Defense Council.

The bailiff led Cado to the witness chair. As he approached, the wireless transmitter under his skin signaled to the court's computer network his identity and the list of charges, which were displayed in the high-definition 3-D hologram for all to see.

The prosecutor reminded the press corps that some of the information that would be presented could affect national security and that since the nation was in a state of war against terrorism, the government would have to approve all content before it could be released to the public. That announcement was for show. The government has full control over the media and censors everything that citizens hear, read, or watch.

Once again, the defendant's memory was accessed via the Life Enhancement Monitor (LEM), a microchip implanted at the base of his brain. The judge instructed the court clerk to program the LEM to perform the necessary stimulation—pursuant to Statute 432c, article one, section 201—to give the government the power to control a person's thoughts and to access a person's memories, all in the name of national security. The LEM's electrical impulses triggered the part of the brain that put the defendant, Johnny Cado, into a state of semiconsciousness, inducing a euphoric feeling that made him able to speak clearly, but also ensured that he could only tell the truth when asked a question. The images from his memory corresponded to his testimony and were simultaneously broadcast, like a motion picture, for the court to see and hear—it was the perfect truth serum.

The prosecutor instructed Cado to begin his testimony where he had left off prior to the court's recess.

Chapter 13:
The Awakening

Everything was dark, black, and deafeningly quiet. I don't recall having any dreams or stirring in my sleep until something aroused my consciousness. My first thoughts were that something was out there in the dark wilderness. I was floating above the earth but slowly sinking toward a dense forest. Something was drawing me down to earth.

There it was again. Something made a sound—maybe it was a foot stepping on a twig. No. Someone said something. Then suddenly, a rush of cold; I hadn't felt anything before, still floating on a cloud in a sea of dark.

What was out there in the dark forest, stirring around? Was that a twig snapping under someone's foot? A colder wind blew over me. I began to shiver and to dream that I was lying naked on an ice plain with a forest in the distance. I couldn't move. I wondered if those were wolves that had noticed me. I felt cold and vulnerable.

The sound was getting closer and becoming clearer. The closer the sound got, the colder I became. Then I heard a woman's voice ever so faintly calling to me from the dark: "Giovanni."

I felt the rush of cold air again, but it was now much colder, shockingly cold down to my core.

Then I heard a distant voice calling out to me: "Johnny…wake up."

Yes, I was certain of it now. Someone familiar was calling my name through the darkness. The cold became unbearable, but then I started to feel something else. Something warm was against me, providing some relief from the bitter cold. Yes, I felt a body, nipples pressed against me; I began to feel aroused.

"Giovanni, please wake up."

That voice! I recognized Angila's voice. It was my sweet Angila's voice calling out to me from the deep, dark wilderness. Each time she called out, I could hear her better, but I became progressively colder at the same time. I became aware that I had been dreaming and that she was trying to wake me. I began to stir. Then I heard her say clearly: "Johnny. I love you. Giovanni, PLEASE wake up for me, Angila. I need you." She alternated using my name given at birth with my Americanized name, not certain which one I would respond to best.

My eyes opened slightly and I could see a faint light. I wondered where I was. I could feel Angila on top of me, making love to me. I was terribly cold, but the sensation of being in her felt better than ever before despite the painful cold that I felt all over. I thought at first that we must be in our bed at home in Paris, but in response to my first movement, she lowered the blanket, exposing our heads.

"Oh my God, can you hear me? Johnny, please tell me that you are all right," she said with a great deal of emotion.

The sudden exposure of my head to the cooler air shocked me enough to make me open my eyes wide. The bright light hurt my eyes, so I quickly closed them again. Angila was still on top of me, kissing my face over and over and whispering into my ear: "Wake up! I love you; I need you." I was enjoying her lovemaking despite the terrible cold. It was sheer ecstasy. I lifted my arms for the first time; my hands felt her back and ass, and I let out a groan that corresponded with my climax.

"Johnny. Can you talk to me?"

"Yes," I whispered.

With that response, I felt her entire body shaking and she began to weep almost hysterically. Despite her crying, I could hear her thanking God for saving me.

In time, I became more alert and began to look around, my eyes still adjusting to the bright light. In between each blink I caught a glimpse of our surroundings. Nearest to the bed was a large, red, glowing heater that blew hot air directly onto my face. I could also feel warm air blowing onto the back of my neck and hear the buzzing of a heater's motor coming from behind me. With a great deal of effort, I lifted my head a little to see past the heater and saw a nurse wearing a white lab coat. My vision became clearer with every blink. There was someone beside me, and behind her! I looked in the opposite direction and saw others.

Instinctively I said: "What the fuck?"

We were in a room full of people watching us have sex! I was suddenly overwhelmed with embarrassment. I was glad that our bodies were still completely covered by several thick blankets, because I was embarrassed by the crowd and because I was still freezing cold—well, actually, I was unfreezing cold. Despite being concealed by blankets, I was sure that it was obvious to all that we had been having sex. My thoughts turned to Angila. She was a virgin when we married and was very modest. This was totally out of character for her—and for me.

The first person I recognized was Professor Hirt. He began to move closer as if he were going to speak. Next to him was Hans Fischer, also known as Scarface, the undercover SS agent who had arrested us in France. There were others there also: nurses and uniformed Nazis, most likely SS men. We were in a clinical setting, and I was being monitored for my heart rate, temperature, and breathing capacity.

"What is going on?" I asked, whispering into Angila's ear so that only she could hear.

"Oh, Johnny. Do you know who I am?"

"What a silly question. Of course! You are my wife, Angila."

The crowd in the room began applauding, and Angila wept. She was overcome with joy and whispered to me, "I have so much to tell you."

Hirt instructed a nurse to provide him with "the patient's vitals."

The nurse responded that my heart rate was normal, my internal body temperature was 28 degrees Celsius, and I was breathing with short, rapid breaths.

Hirt instructed a technician to adjust the fan speed so that it didn't blow with full force. Another nurse handed Angila a robe, which she slipped into while continuing to conceal herself with the blankets. Then she stood by the bed wearing only a robe.

I looked at her with amazement and asked, "Did you know these people were here, watching us?"

"Yes, darling. It had to be done. We will be alone soon and I will explain. You will understand."

My eyelids felt heavy and I felt myself beginning to nod off to sleep.

Hirt instructed his staff to take his patient to a room so that I could recover.

I was still sleepy, and seconds before I fell asleep, Hirt moved closer and I heard him say to Angila: "Once again, you've done a fine job, my dear."

The next thing that I remember was being in what appeared to be a hospital room.

Angila was there. For the first time, I noticed something different about her. She was thinner, frailer, and her long, beautiful, black hair was frazzled with split ends and cut shorter than it had been when we were separated in France. Her eyes were sunken, and my beautiful angel looked as if she had aged by ten years.

She crawled into the bed to lie beside me. I had fallen in love with Angila the moment that I first saw her in Sicily. Her youthful energy and excitability made her a joy to be around, but she was also a real woman—a good person with a loving, kind heart. She was always doing for and thinking of others before she considered her own wants or needs. She was loyal and committed to her wedding vows. At this moment, I realized that I loved her more than ever, which caused feelings of guilt to overcome me. This beautiful, wonderful woman deserved a better life than what I had given her. She deserved to live in a house with a picket fence and to worry only about caring for her husband and future children. I had failed her as a husband. I promised God that someway, somehow, someday, I would make things right with her if he would give me a chance.

Hirt asked if I could sit upright, but I was too weak to do so without help. It was still very cold—in some ways colder than before—so I didn't want any part of my body exposed to the room temperature—not even my big toe. Earmuffs muffled sounds but kept my ears warm.

"Here, give us a hand," Hirt said to a nurse, and the two of them pulled my arms to lift me enough so that another nurse could place a pillow behind my back.

Hirt asked me a series of questions to test my memory. He told me to state my name and age.

"Johnny Cado or Cicero Friddi, take your pick. I'm forty-three years old. Born in Sicily in 1899."

Hirt smiled and asked, "What day is it today?"

I couldn't answer that question. "I'm not sure, maybe Wednesday?"

"What year is it?"

I paused for a second to think. "1942," I replied.

Hirt looked at Hans and they both smiled. Then Hirt looked into my eyes with a medical instrument and inspected my ears, mouth, and throat. He listened to my heart and lungs as I took deep, slow breaths.

The nurses left, leaving just Angila, Hans, and Hirt in the room with me. Hans silently observed.

Hirt checked my temperature repeatedly. Once he was satisfied that it was close to normal, he instructed me to stand. I complied. He gave me a battery of tests, such as requiring me to stretch my arms parallel to the floor and alternate touching my nose with one hand and then the other. He gave me an eye exam, in which I read the letters from a chart several feet away. Once satisfied, he instructed me to return to my bed.

"He has recovered remarkably well, but we will need to keep him under close observation to see if there are any residual effects that we cannot detect at this time. After a few days, if all goes well, the two of you can go home together," he said to Angila.

"Can somebody tell me what happened?" I pleaded.

"Herr Cado, we are in the Dachau Medical Research Center. Can you tell me how you came to be here? What you did yesterday? Tell me everything that you remember about recent events," Hirt responded.

It took me a few minutes to recall yesterday's events. Running my fingers through my hair as if it would help me think better, it came to me.

"I remember opening the pantry door and walking down the flight of stairs to my hidden wine cellar. Then I opened the secret door that led to the outside, where Drago and his wife were waiting for me. We traded house keys, disguises, and identities before saying our goodbyes. Next I remember the train ride to the French demarcation line and the feeling that Angila and I were free at last. I remember being betrayed by Rocko, and the terrible feeling of hopelessness and despair that I had on the return trip to Paris."

I remembered, but didn't express to Hirt, the fear that I felt when I arrived at Dachau and the terrible images of that man in the decompression chamber, tearing at his face, ripping out his hair, and banging his head on the glass—trying anything to stop the pain before he exploded into a bloody mess.

"I remember being bound in a straitjacket and begging for mercy, crying, and feeling completely helpless," I said as I glared at Hirt. "I remember that you injected me with something that made me fall asleep," I continued.

Then I demanded to know what they had done to me.

My thoughts turned to Angila. "What did they do to you?" I asked her.

She placed her hand on my cheek and said softly, "Nothing. They did not do anything to me."

I could tell that she was lying to me, so I wondered what hard truth she was protecting me from. Whatever it was caused her to appear as if she had aged ten years overnight. Her hand that touched my cheek was rough, unlike the soft hands that I recalled. For a moment, I began to doubt if she was the real Angila. Could this be a test to see if an Angila imposter could fool me? I remembered sitting at the dinner table in New York, fooling Ben Siegel, Vito Genovese, and others into thinking that I was Lucky Luciano. I observed Angila and thought of the differences in how I remembered her. First of all, Angila would never be so immodest as to have sex in a room with other people watching, even if our bodies were covered. She was too proper to even discuss sex with anyone—even with me. Sure, sex was good, but she would blush whenever I said anything sexually provocative. Her hair and hands were different. She was thinner, almost skin and bones. She had always been affectionate, but seemed more so than ever. Most noticeable were the concern in her eyes and the maturity of her demeanor. This woman wasn't the child who had married me. I thought there was no way that this was my Angila dand wondered how to handle my suspicions. The terrifying question came to mind: if she is not the real Angila, then where is my wife? A more rational question came to me: what would be the benefit of having a double for Angila? A few moments before, I had felt the strongest love I had ever felt for her. Did I have those feelings for an impersonator? I had to know.

"Angila?"

"Yes, my love."

"Do you recall our first date?" I watched her eyes and expression carefully as she answered.

"Of course. How could I ever forget?" She smiled and patted my hand.

"Tell me about it."

"Do you not remember?"

"No. Please tell me," I lied.

"You were so polite—such a gentleman. You invited my mamma and papà to go with us to the opera. You and Papà both fell asleep. Then afterward Mamma and I cooked spaghetti, and you flipped your plate into your lap. You were so embarrassed, but I thought you were adorable."

"That's exactly right. I remember now," I said happily, convinced that she was my Angila.

I turned my gaze to Hirt. "What did you do to me? And what have you done to Angila?"

"We have not harmed you or her. We've taken good care of your wife, Angila," Hirt replied.

"What do you mean, you've taken good care of her? How long have I been asleep?"

"How long do you think you've been asleep?" Hirt answered with a question, frustrating me.

It seemed to me as if I had just awakened from a normal night's sleep, but I needed answers. "Please do not answer my question with a question," I pleaded.

Hans stepped forward for the first time to speak. "You have performed a valuable service for the fatherland. Your contribution to science will contribute to the survival of the Third Reich and the Fuehrer is aware of this and is personally grateful," he said.

"Will someone answer my questions with a straight answer?" I was becoming more frustrated by the second.

Seeing this, Angila would not allow me to anguish any longer. She placed her hand on my face, kissed my cheek, and then said to me,

"My darling, they froze you for almost three years. It's 1945!"

Chapter 14:
Angila's Journey

"Why did your wife collaborate with the Nazis while you were in a frozen coma?"

I was fortunate that I had been given anesthesia prior to being frozen; everyone who had been frozen without anesthesia did not survive.

Over the next couple of weeks, except for the routine interruptions for meals, examinations, and daily monitored exercises, Angila and I were left to ourselves in my hospital room. At first, she didn't want to tell me everything that had happened to her—the things she was forced to do while I was frozen solid. But in the end, little by little, I heard her entire story.

Like me, she had been taken straight to Dachau from the gestapo headquarters after being arrested in France. The gestapo agents were instructed to take her directly to the mad Dr. Rascher's office upon her arrival. He explained to her the gravity of her situation.

"The penalty for supporting the enemy in a time of war is death," Rascher told her. "But if you are fortunate enough to have a compassionate judge, you may be spared death. But at best, you face hard labor for the remainder of your life," he told Angila with an evil smile.

"But in situations such as these," he continued, "the Dachau Medical Center can appropriate a prisoner to be used as a test patient for one of its various medical experiments.

You can thank me for sparing your life by selecting you to serve as a test patient."

Dr. Rascher took Angila on a guided tour of his madhouse. Adjoining the clinical-looking building—which was claimed to be a medical research facility for the good of science and mankind—was a concentration camp for prisoners of war, Jews, political prisoners, and anyone else that the Germans chose to incarcerate. The conditions were appalling. It was obvious that the prisoners working in the fields were grossly malnourished. The women were separated from the men by a tall fence topped with barbed wire.

Angila told me that she would "never forget the look that one woman, about my age, gave me as we made eye contact. It was as though she was begging for my help without saying a word."

She had seen a dead, male prisoner hanging by his neck, in plain view for all to see. This was a warning to those who might consider breaking the rules. She saw a line of women and girls, stripped completely naked, waiting for their turn to enter a bathhouse. She saw a woman on her knees, her hands bound to a post above her head, being whipped by a German soldier. She was so near to death that she no longer cried out in pain when the whip tore her flesh. Rascher scolded Angila each time she tried to look away from the pain and carnage, insisting that she see everything.

After the gruesome tour of the death camp, she and Rascher returned to the sterile medical facility, where professional nurses dressed in all-white uniforms were in stark contrast to the dirty concentration camp run by the SS. The tour continued.

"This medical facility is conducting the world's most advanced research programs in a variety of disciplines," Rascher said to Angila.

They entered a section of the building that featured a long, wide hall with large panes of glass on each side providing Angila with a view of the test patients in each room. Rascher pointed to a man sitting in a chair, dressed in prison stripes, his bare arm extended so the nurse could locate a vein for injection.

"This is where we are making advances in the area of disease control. That man was sentenced to death, so instead of wasting his life by hanging him, we have injected him with a dose of typhus. He will still die, but instead of dying a useless death, he will have contributed to science. This is much more humane and beneficial to mankind," said Rascher.

Within minutes of the injection, the man was foaming at the mouth and kicking his bound feet—as much as he could.

Angila was sickened, and could not keep herself from telling Rascher that he was a demented man.

"You should remember that we have your husband! He could be that man in there if I chose. Never forget that his treatment—as well as your own—depends on whether you please me," Rascher replied.

That was the first clue as to what Rascher had in mind for my wife.

Another wing of the hospital was dedicated to "psychoanalysis." Test patients were given a wide variety of hallucinogenic drugs in various doses in order for the staff to monitor the effects. Some of the patients were confined, either by straitjacket or by being strapped to a bed, but some were allowed to move about freely in their padded room. Rascher explained that the glass windows were four inches thick and could not be broken by the strongest of men. Angila's heart ached for these men. Some thrashed around the best they could within their constraints. Some sat still, staring off into space as if they were mindless zombies. Others laughed, some cried, and some threw violent fits, crashing into the glass until blood covered their faces. Some died instantly from heart failure. Angila pleaded with Rascher to stop making her witness the torture. He refused.

Next, Rascher showed her the gruesome pressure chamber experiments. I can attest that one viewing of this can make even a tough man cringe. I'm certain that Angila was permanently scarred from seeing a screaming man explode before her eyes, but it was so horrible that she couldn't talk about it. She didn't have to—I recall all too well that horrible chamber.

Lastly, Rascher took her to the section of the facility where the freezing experiments took place.

"The most important research program in the world is taking place here, for this could guarantee the continuation of the Third Reich well into the future," Rascher explained.

By now, Angila was emotionally drained. She thought that she was numb to any more shock, but she was wrong. Standing at one end of the hall, he explained that the test patients on the right had been given anesthesia and the patients on the left had not. They entered the first room on the left, where they inspected a glass coffin containing a frozen stiff.

"Notice how his eyes and mouth are wide open?" Rascher asked.

The man's face was contorted. Angila surmised that he was in pain when his heart stopped.

Rascher led her to the next room, where Professor Hirt and two orderlies were about to perform a "procedure" on a test patient. The naked man was forced to lie in a tub of ice. Hirt and Rascher used their hands to submerge the man. Hirt instructed a nurse to insert a thermometer into his anus.

"Don't look away!" Rascher yelled at Angila. The man repeatedly screamed out in pain and cursed his tormentors. He was almost entirely submerged in icy water, except for his nose and mouth. After a long while he stopped making any sound at all. He looked as if he were dead.

Angila asked Rascher why he insisted that she witness these things and told him that she would rather hang than see any more. He ignored her pleading and took her to another room on the other side of the hall. There was a glass coffin, filled with a block of ice and the body of a naked man.

"I've seen enough. Why do you continue to torture me this way?" she pleaded with Rascher once again.

"Look closer, dear. This is the face of a man who was given anesthesia before being frozen. Observe the peaceful look on his face?" Rascher replied.

Angila looked in that direction, but she didn't really look at the man's face.

"Look at his face!" Rascher yelled.

She obeyed and saw the worst thing that she had seen all day. The frozen face was mine. Angila screamed and turned to Rascher and attacked him like a lioness trying to protect her cubs. The orderlies helped Rascher to subdue her. Then he told her that if she wanted to see her husband alive again, she would control her temper and never make him "unhappy again."

Hirt entered the room holding a prisoner by the arm and called Angila's attention to him.

"This man was frozen for six months, and he now stands before you in perfect health," Hirt explained.

"Your husband could be standing before you as well, if you obey orders," Rascher told Angila.

"Your husband will be all right. They used anesthesia on me too. It was if I had gone to sleep one night and woke up the following day," the test patient said in broken English.

This gave Angila hope that I could be saved. Seeing that she had calmed down, Rascher told the orderlies to release Angila and then he told her that he had a proposition to make to her. He led her to his office and ordered her to sit.

"The way that I see it you have two choices. You can serve the Reich by being a test patient in the experiment of my choosing, or you can work for me as my personal assistant. If you choose to be my assistant, you will be treated well so long as you please me at all times. If you do this, you will get to see your husband alive once more. If not, you will both die in my most creative experiment. It is your choice. I don't want you to accept the position as my assistant unless you are enthusiastic about it and can convince me that you are happy pleasing me. Now, what will it be?" Rascher's eyes undressed Angila as he explained her options.

She had no choice and he knew it. She thought of me and realized that the only chance that she had to save me was to serve Rascher. She swallowed her pride and told him that she would serve him with enthusiasm.

"Excellent! Now take off your clothes," the sadistic Dr. Rascher demanded.

Angila was a good Catholic woman. Virtue was important to her, but she was still reeling from the emotional turmoil caused by the sights and sounds of the day, and he gave her no time to think.

"Do not hesitate. Off with your clothes at once!"

She imagined my face on the man who foamed at the mouth after being injected with typhus and obeyed her cruel master. With tear-filled eyes, she dropped her dress to the floor. I'm sure the bastard was pleased by her beautiful young body. He stood up from his chair and moved from behind the desk. She looked straight ahead fearing what might happen next. He moved close to her and leaned forward to cup her breasts. She stepped back and asked him to please respect her marriage vows.

In the coldest of voices, Rascher explained to her that she had to act as if she lusted after him and beg him for sex as often as he wanted—otherwise, he would think of an especially painful experiment to perform on her and her husband.

"I can be very creative, if you haven't noticed. For example, it might be fun to see how long it would take for a frozen man to explode in a pressure chamber." Seeing that she understood the hopelessness of the situation, he said to her in a cruel tone, "Now, beg for me."

Angila broke down and wept when she told me this, and begged me to forgive her for breaking her vow to me. She told me that she would understand if I wanted to divorce her. "I am dirty," she said.

At first, I was angry—not at Angila but at Rascher. I wanted to kill him. Then I realized that Angila thought that I was angry with her.

I am not ashamed to tell you that I began to cry also, but I quickly told her that I did not want a divorce, that I loved her and loved that she was willing to sacrifice herself to save me. "You did what you had to do to survive and to save me. You did not break your vow to me. You were raped. You have nothing to be ashamed of. It is not your fault. It's my fault for not protecting you."

She told me that she wasn't certain if I would still feel that way after I heard the rest of the story. After having his way with her in his office, he informed her that she would be living in his home with his wife.

"You will serve as our servant when you are not working here at the Research Center," Rascher said.

They arrived by limousine at his mansion that afternoon.

"You are to serve her as you serve me," he said as he introduced his wife, Nini, as Mrs. Rascher.

Mrs. Rascher was nearly as hard and cruel as her husband. She spoke condescendingly to Angila as if she were subhuman. Sometimes, she would flick her cigarette ashes onto the floor and scream at Angila for not cleaning them up quick enough to suit her.

Angila was given a tiny room in the servants' quarters on the third floor of the huge mansion. She closed the door and threw herself onto the bed. Alone for the first time since our arrest in France, she cried herself to sleep, only to be awakened by nightmares throughout the night.

As instructed, she was dressed in her uniform and in the kitchen preparing breakfast for the Raschers by five o'clock the next morning. She wasn't alone though. Kamila and Zofia introduced themselves. Like Angila, they were young, beautiful, Catholic girls and were there against their will. Kamila was the youngest at about twenty-two and had been there the longest. Zofia was twenty-five—three years older than Kamila and nearly three years younger than Angila.

The women, particularly Zofia, were pillars of strength in a sea of evil. Despite having been raped numerous times and having their dignities stripped in every way imaginable, they remained strong in their Christian faith.

After the brief introductions Zofia instructed them to come together to close their eyes, bow their heads, and pray.

"Quickly, before the devil returns," Zofia instructed.

Angila and Kamila obeyed.

"Dear God, please project Angila from the evil in this house and this country. Protect her spirit, show your love for her, and help her separate herself from her body," Zofia prayed aloud.

This was the first sign of goodness that Angila had seen since she couldn't remember when. She hugged Zofia and thanked her. "I cannot express to you how much I needed to hear that," Angila said.

"I know, dear. We are here for you always," Zofia said reassuringly, and Kamila nodded in agreement.

Zofia's faith saved my wife's life—therefore, she saved my life also.

Suddenly they heard movement in the living quarters, causing them to spring into action. This was a new experience for Angila, but the other girls showed her what was expected.

"The Master's wife does not want anything to eat in the mornings but must have hot coffee and does not want to be kept waiting. Dr. Rascher wants his breakfast served in bed," Kamila explained.

Angila followed Zofia into the living quarters, observing her technique of serving Mrs. Rascher. Then she followed Kamila to serve Dr. Rascher his breakfast. Rascher was sitting up in bed waiting to be served. Angila watched as Kamila placed his tray in his lap. Rascher grabbed Kamila's arm and then—looking at Angila to ensure that she was watching—let go of her arm and cupped her breast with his hand. Kamila did not flinch. She looked forward, expressionless. This wasn't a new experience for her. Then he slapped her on her ass and said: "Tell Fritz to have my car ready by seven." Then he looked at Angila. "Get out of that uniform and be dressed and ready to accompany me to work by seven."

Angila rode in the front seat with the driver while Rascher rode in the back. He lived only minutes from the house of horrors, which is what Angila called the Dachau Medical Research Center. The driver, Fritz, opened the door for Rascher. Fritz told Angila to walk behind Rascher at all times.

Angila was instructed to wait for Rascher in a sitting room while he tended to things in his office. Hours later he returned and said: "Your job will be to work with me in the freezing experiments program. I am certain this will please you, as you have a particular interest in the subject. Today, you will see how we wake someone from a deep-frozen sleep."

Angila was interested in this subject. She needed to know if I could truly be saved. Rascher led her to a room with comfortable chairs that circled the room on an elevated platform. Angila was instructed to sit to Rascher's right. The other chairs in the room began to fill. Female assistants sat in every other chair, in between male staff members. From this position, everyone had a clear view of the floor below, which featured a bed surrounded by electric heaters. Next to the bed was a tub of hot water, and next to the tub of water was a glass coffin containing a man enclosed in a block of ice. There were two female nurses and two male technicians on the floor taking directions from Professor Hirt. There were others on the floor performing a variety of functions. Keeping their distance so as to not be in the way of the other workers on the floor were two women, wearing nothing more than bathrobes and house slippers. Angila was curious as to their role.

After receiving the signal from Rascher to begin, the male technicians grabbed hold of the end handles on the coffin and lifted the frozen block of ice, removing the man from the glass coffin. They gently lowered the block of ice into the warming tub.

That was the cue for two women—presumably prisoners—to remove their bathrooms and take their positions on the bed. Angila blushed at their apparent lack of modesty. She had never seen anything of this sort before and looked around to see the expressions on the faces of the other spectators. The others didn't seem to be surprised by the display of public nudity.

The hot water melted the block of ice containing the human figure. Once the ice was completely melted away, and the man's body was no longer completely rigid, his body was placed on the bed next to the two naked women. A nurse walked over to the bed and inserted a thermometer into his anus to monitor the man's temperature. The nurse backed away and the two naked women took their positions on either side of the unconscious man. The women were light skinned, unlike Angila. She guessed that they were from eastern Europe. They pressed their naked bodies against the test patient and began rubbing their hands over his face and body, but were quickly hidden from view by a blanket placed over them by the nurses. More blankets were added, and the heating fans were turned to the highest setting.

The threesome were completely hidden by the blanket, but it was obvious from the movement of the blanket that they were fondling the frozen man. After thirty minutes or so of this, despite being concealed by the blankets, it was apparent that one of the women was on top of the man having sex with him. Angila looked away, embarrassed that she was witnessing this.

"We've tried many techniques, but we've learned that this procedure is the most effective for returning a man's internal temperature to normal without causing damage to his vital organs," Rascher whispered to Angila.

Angila noticed that the others in the audience seemed to be enjoying the sexual performance taking place on the floor. It was the most perverted thing that she had ever witnessed. She wondered how people could do this in public. Did they have no shame? Rascher noticed the disgusted look on Angila's face and—for no other reason than to humiliate her—he forcefully placed her hand on his crotch and reminded her of the ramifications of not making him happy. Angila remembered the awful things that she had witnessed in this very building, so despite her disgust and embarrassment, she followed orders and fondled Rascher while he watched the two women thaw the frozen man. It was plain to her that this was a routine event among this group, because the few who noticed what she was doing to Rascher reacted as if this were a common occurrence. This made her feel sick to her stomach, but she dared not to show her disgust.

Rascher stood, zipping his trousers, and walked down to the floor to join Professor Hirt and his team. Angila was glad that her job was finished for the moment and took this opportunity to pray to God for forgiveness and guidance. She was truly in the valley of the shadow of death.

The movements taking place underneath the blankets increased. Angila knew the effect of cold on a man's performance and wondered how the man was responding physically. One of the women pulled the blanket back and yelled something in German, and the crowd applauded. After a brief inspection of the man, Rascher whispered to a nurse. The nurse nodded and left the floor to approach Angila. "Dr. Rascher has requested that you join him on the floor," the nurse said.

The nurse led Angila to the floor where Rascher and Hirt were talking to the patient. Rascher pulled Angila to his side so that she could hear their conversation.

"How long have you been asleep?" Rascher asked the man.

"I don't know. I suppose a few minutes—maybe fifteen?" the dazed man responded. He was shocked to learn that he had been frozen for nine months.

"I want you to stay close to this patient and learn the procedures that we go through to monitor his health," Rascher said to Angila.

Angila rode in the front seat with the driver on the way to the Rascher mansion. It was now time for her second job—serving as one of the Rascher's domestic servants. She was the new meat in the house, and Rascher had an unquenchable sexual appetite. While dinner was being prepared, he walked into the kitchen, walked up to Angila from behind and grabbed both ass cheeks, not caring that Zofia and Kamila were watching. "I want to taste you for desert," he said as he groped her ass.

When Rascher left the kitchen, Zofia gave Angila rosary beads and made the sign of the cross with her hand. "Remember always: you are not your flesh," Zofia said.

Angila was relieved when Dr. Rascher drank so much wine with his dinner that he was too sleepy to have other thoughts.

Zofia, Kamila, and Angila gathered in Kamila's room that evening—the first of many such meetings. Angila felt a special bond with these women. They became the sisters that she had never had. She imagined that this room was in a home far away, in another country, and that they were a happy family, there to discuss the loves of their lives. In a desperate attempt to think of better times, Angila suggested that they all take turns describing the happiest times in their past. Zofia began.

"The happiest time of my life was the day that I was married to Edvard. He was the most beautiful man and a kind and good man. The whole village attended the wedding. There were so many that a crowd formed outside of the church, unable to enter because the church was already filled. My father escorted me, and my mother was so proud. My little brother, Dominik, was at the wedding too. After the wedding we could not afford to go on a honeymoon, so Mr. Novak, the town's innkeeper, gave us a room for one week as a wedding present. I lived in a beautiful town with the happiest people. Edvard was a carpenter and he could repair anything. He could cook! And he could kiss."

The girls giggled like adolescents. It felt good to Angila to feel innocent again, even if it was make-believe. The smile faded from Zofia's face, and her eyes filled with tears as she continued.

"We were making love when the Germans pounded on our door. We could not afford our own home, so we lived with my family."

"Zofia, you do not have to tell us. Remember happy times," Angila interrupted.

"I must. It was a Sunday and my mother and father and Dominik were in church. The same church where we were married. Edvard and I should have been there too, but he had worked late into the night trying to finish repairing a neighbor's roof before the next rain, so we decided to sleep late and to miss church for the first time since we met. The Germans kicked open the door to our house and entered when no one answered. This startled us, so Edvard jumped to his feet and put on his pants to see what was the matter. German soldiers pointed guns at him, and another entered our bedroom and forced me at gunpoint to come with him.

They would not allow me to put on my clothes. Edvard tried to come to my aid, so they shot him in the head. My heart was broken, but they would not let me grieve or go to him. They dragged me down the street to where the church was burning. The doors had been chained, and I could hear the screams. I knew that my family was in there. The Germans went to every house and brought everyone in the town who was not in church out into the street. They separated us into two groups. The women and children and boys under fifteen were in one group, and all men and boys fifteen and older were lined up in another group facing German soldiers who pointed their machine guns at them." Zofia paused and noticed that Angila and Kamila were listening intently with tear filled eyes.

"One of the soldiers—he may have been a general—spoke over a loudspeaker and said that this town was the home of a criminal who had murdered a high-ranking officer in the Third Reich. The Fuehrer had ordered our town to cease to exist. Under German law, the name of our town may never be mentioned, nor shall it be printed. All books referencing our town had to be destroyed. Its men would be killed, and its women and children would be relocated to labor camps" she continued.

All three women were sobbing by this time. "He said that if the men accepted their fate, the women and children would be spared. He said that for every man who ran or resisted, ten women would be killed. The men stood there and accepted their fate. Not one single man ran away. They were executed before our eyes. Next, the Germans placed chains on our legs connecting all of the women and children together like cattle. They led us to the edge of town and made us watch as demolition crews destroyed my town." Zofia wiped the tears from her eyes and cleared her throat. "They burned every home and building. Within the span of one day, every bit of debris was dumped into a deep pit and covered. At the very end, trees were planted and grass seed was spread over the scarred earth. My town no longer existed. We were led away in different directions," Zofia explained.

The three women held each other tightly and sobbed. Then Kamila began telling her story.

"I have never been married, but I have been in love. His name was Jakub. We never made love. I was a virgin until the Germans took that from me. I was living in Warsaw when the Germans invaded and tried to escape with my family, but we were captured. I cannot remember any good times," Kamila said in the saddest of tones.

Angila lowered her head, sad that her plan to escape reality had failed.

"What happened to Jakub?" Zofia asked.

"He bravely joined the Polish Army to fight the Germans, but I never heard from him after he left for battle," Kamila replied, trying to hold back tears.

Zofia asked Angila to tell her story, but before she began, they heard footsteps coming up the stairs, so they scattered to their individual rooms. It was Dr. Rascher. He announced loudly as he approached the top of the stairs, as if unconcerned that his wife might hear: "Who is the lovely that will satisfy me tonight?" From the hall and through the closed bedroom doors he could be heard: "Eeny, meeny, miny, moe."

Angila cringed with guilt because she was relieved when he chose Kamila's room and not hers.

The following day, Angila learned more about her duties in the freezing experiments. It was now wintertime, which gave Rascher more opportunities to freeze people. The temperature was well below freezing. Two naked prisoners were strapped to a gurney outdoors in the bitter cold. They were not afforded the luxury of anesthesia, and Angila was instructed to pour ice water on them, one at a time, until they froze. This she couldn't do—even if it meant certain death for her and for me. She told me that she believed that I would understand. I told her that I agreed with her decision.

Rascher was furious. The men were doused with ice water by some of his more cooperative staff, but to teach her a lesson, he ordered the SS to deliver a dozen prisoners from the concentration camp to him for a special project.

The men were all frail and weak, resembling skeletons more than men. One by one, they were marched into one of the experimental rooms while Angila was made to watch.

"Today's experiment is to determine the effects of a substance which aids in blood clotting, which will reduce bleeding from gunshot wounds during combat or during surgery. Each subject has taken a Polygal tablet," Rascher announced.

There was a gasp when Rascher produced a handgun. He turned and shot the unsuspecting man in the neck, then looked at his watch to time his death. Angila winced at the cruelty.

The second man was led into the room. An orderly announced that he had taken a Polygal tablet an hour sooner than the first test patient. Rascher instructed the orderly to amputate the man's arm, without anesthesia. The man screamed in pain and bled to death in front of Angila's eyes.

UnLucky Double

A dozen men all died similar painful, gruesome deaths, while Angila was forced to watch. That was the first part of her punishment for disobeying a direct order. She received the balance of her punishment at the Rascher residence later that evening. As soon as the Raschers finished dinner, Dr. Rascher had Angila on his mind. He told his wife that he had business to attend to with the servants, and she remained downstairs in the living quarters while he led the three women upstairs.

"Angila failed to obey a direct order today. What is the punishment for disobeying an officer of the Third Reich?" said Rascher in a loud, commanding tone.

Zofia held her rosary beads tightly, and Kamila started crying. Angila, still numb from seeing a dozen men die gruesome deaths that day, could not imagine anything worse than that she had already seen. She thought that she was ready to die. Rascher grabbed the rosary beads from Zofia's hands and ripped her shirt, exposing her breasts.

"No! Please punish me! I am the one that did wrong," screamed Angila.

"Yes, you were wrong to disobey me, and this is all your fault," Rascher said as he slapped Zofia, causing her to tumble onto the bed. Rascher reached his hands up Zofia's skirt and removed her underpants. Then his pants dropped to the floor.

Angila unbuttoned her shirt and exposed her breasts. "Please, take me. I will make you happier," she said.

Rascher smiled but ignored Angila and turned Zofia face down before mounting her. Zofia clasped her hands together, as if praying, while being brutally raped from behind.

Witnessing this hurt Angila more than if she had been raped. She and Kamila cried and pleaded for Rascher to stop, but he seemed to enjoy hearing their pleading most of all.

That night, after the Raschers had gone to sleep and every night thereafter, the three women met in Angila's room to pray and to comfort one another. "You are not your flesh," Angila said to Zofia.

Rascher wasn't finished punishing Angila. The following day he announced that there would be another awakening that afternoon. Angila stood next to Rascher watching the experienced staff preparing the room. Rascher held a clipboard. The water in the tub was heated; the fans were strategically placed around the bed. People began to fill the spectator chairs. A blond German nurse approached and extended a bathrobe for Angila. Instinctively she took the robe, then looked at Rascher questioningly. Her stomach churned when he explained that she would be one of the two women that would thaw the frozen man. This was too much for Angila, who nearly fainted at the thought. Before she could recover from the shocking news, the nurse was leading her by the arm to the dressing room, where she was instructed to remove her clothes and put on the bathrobe and house slippers.

There was another woman in the room. She was wearing a matching bathrobe. Angila recognized her as one of the two women who had awakened the last frozen man. She was in her early thirties and appeared to be well nourished, but not overweight. Angila sat in the chair across from the other woman and began to sob. The daily routine of being exposed to shocking evil, seeing people tortured, murdered, and raped—and now being forced to have public sex—was overwhelming. She thought of suicide, but her thoughts were interrupted by the other woman who asked, *"Verstehen Sie?"*

Living among the Germans for two years had enabled Angila to understand their language far better than she could speak it. "No. Italiano, English, or Francais," she replied.

The woman affectionately placed her hand on Angila's hand. "Hello. I Talia. No cry," she said in broken English.

Fighting back her tears, Angila looked at the woman's face and saw kindness in her eyes and a loving smile on her face. She wondered what kind of woman could perform sex on a stranger in front of a crowd of strangers and live with herself afterward with no shame. She had assumed the women participants had been prostitutes.

"You do good. My husband…" She struggled to find the words and tried to use her hands and body to explain. "Husband cold. You help," said Talia.

Angila understood. "Oh God, the frozen man is your husband?"

"*Ja.* Yes." The woman was pleased to see that Angila understood. "Help me. Please. I beg."

This changed everything. This woman was trying to save her husband's life. As always, Angila applied her Christian beliefs to the situation. She asked herself, "If that were my husband out there frozen, would I want another woman's help in trying to save him?"

The answer was clear to her. She wiped away her tears, hugged the woman, and told her in German that she understood; then in English she said, "I will help you."

The woman showed her gratitude by returning the hug and kissing her on the cheek. Angila replaced her clothes with the bathrobe and slippers. The two women walked hand in hand to take their place on the floor. Angila kept her eyes on the floor, trying to forget the crowd of spectators.

The frozen man was lifted and placed into the tub of heated water. The ice block began to melt away. Talia mumbled something, presumably a prayer. It took twenty minutes or so for the warm water to thaw the man sufficiently to proceed to the next step. One nurse spoke to Talia in German and the other spoke to Angila in English: "Drop your robes and take your positions beside the bed."

Talia, still holding Angila's hand, led the way. The two were instructed where to stand. Talia dropped her robe. Angila hesitated. Talia turned to her and gently pulled the drawstring and removed her robe for her. "For my Dimitri," she said.

Instinctively, Angila covered her privates the best that she could, but one of the male technicians grabbed her arms and forcefully removed her hands. He pointed to the cameraman who was a few feet away. Suddenly there was a flash: a record was to be made of this event, adding to her humiliation. She didn't recall seeing the women being photographed before. Talia was the first to take her place next to the frozen body on the bed. Taking her signal from Talia, Angila entered from the opposite side of the bed. She drew back instinctively upon feeling the man's icy cold skin. He felt dead. Talia's legs were wrapped around the man's right leg. Her upper body covered one side of the man's chest. Her face pressed to his, cheek to cheek, she said to Angila, "Please."

Angila mimicked her by covering as much of the man with her body as possible. The blankets were placed over them, concealing them from the rest of the room, but more importantly, capturing their body heat for use in their important mission.

Talia rubbed the man's chest, neck, and face with her hand. She worked her legs to and fro, creating heat with friction. Angila did the same. They could hear the sound of the electric motors and the spinning fans that blew heated air from all directions toward the trio.

Talia kissed Dimitri's face and talked to him in his native tongue. *"Dimitri. Bitte aufwachen. Ich liebe dich. Ich brauche dich. Wake fur mich, Tailia."*

She repeated these words so often that Angila could recite them verbatim. Later, Talia explained that the words meant, "Dimitri, please wake up. I love you. I need you. Wake up for me, Talia."

An hour or so later, the man's heart began to pump and he started breathing. He was still cool, but no longer as icy cold as before. This was Talia's signal to direct her attention to the man's genitals. Talia fondled Dimitri's privates for at least thirty minutes before the man's body responded. Angila noticed that his breaths were deeper and she could hear his heart beating better than before. By now, it was stifling hot underneath the covers. Angila could still hear the buzzing heater fan motors that surrounded the bed. The heating coils burned a bright red, providing a faint light even under the three blankets that covered the trio. The bed sheets were soaked with sweat.

Dimitri's body no longer felt cold to the touch, but he was not sweating. When Talia felt the time was right, she positioned herself on top of her husband and began making love to him. Angila had to reposition herself to make room for Talia to perform. She pressed Dimitri's head between her breasts and wrapped her arm around the top of his head, trying to provide warmth to his brain. All the while, Talia continued to call out his name and beg him to wake up, but her pleas were interrupted by her groans and gasps for breath. For the first time, Dimitri moved. Instinctively, he lifted his pelvis. Angila's heart raced. She wanted to call out, to ask Talia if she had felt it too, but it was obvious that she had. After that first movement, Talia raised the volume of her voice and with a half cry half laugh she yelled Dimitri's name and in German shouted, *"Wake up!"*

With that, he raised his arms, placed his hands on her hips, and began to thrust his pelvis to and fro—although not with a lot of gusto. Angila and Talia were filled with hope. He was alive! Now their goal was for him to gain consciousness. Talia increased her rhythm, which required her to sit more upright. Realizing that Talia was unable to talk to Dimitri as before, Angila began talking to Dimitri: "Wake up, darling Dimitri, your beautiful wife needs you to wake up. Wake up for Talia." She repeated this several times, alternating between English, Italian, and German, although her German was very poor and she was certain that she wasn't saying it properly. The next thing to move was the man's jaw. He opened his mouth as if to say something, but no words were spoken. Then his head moved a little. Then Dimitri let out a groan and despite the darkness underneath the blankets, Angila saw that his eyes were opened wide. Tears of joy filled her eyes. Talia leaned forward and said something in German that Angila did not understand, but she understood the emotion—joy.

Dimitri spoke for the first time, but it was also in German, so Angila did not comprehend. Her understanding of German was improving with each day, but she had a long way to go before she could carry on a conversation in that dreadful land. Talia answered Dimitri and then leaned back and removed the heavy blankets enough to expose their heads.

Angila had been so focused on saving the love of Talia's life that she had temporarily forgotten where she was, but the removal of the blanket from her head made her aware once again that they were the objects of attention for a crowd of spectators. Thankfully, she could not see past the glow of the heaters or the bright lights that allowed German researchers to film this important "research."

Seemingly from nowhere, Professor Hirt's face appeared only inches from Dimitri's face. Hirt asked him, in German, if he could understand.

Dimitri was startled and was obviously confused. He didn't expect to see another man while he was in bed making love to his wife. With a bewildered expression he thrashed his head from side to side, trying to make sense of his surroundings—and then noticed Angila for the first time.

"Was ist los?" Dimitri spoke in German loud enough that the microphone hanging from above was able to broadcast his voice throughout the small auditorium. The crowd erupted with applause.

Talia placed her hands on each side of his face, forcing him to look only at her. Eye to eye, she whispered to him to remain calm and that she would explain everything to him.

A female nurse tapped on Angila's shoulder to gain her attention. She instructed Angila to put on the bathrobe that she was holding. She started to get out of bed to comply with the nurse's instruction, but Talia stopped her momentarily. "Thank you, Angila. My Dimitri, thank you," Tailia said in English.

Angila enjoyed a moment of pride, a feeling of accomplishment, and happiness for the couple, but upon standing up to put on her robe, she saw a photographer filming her naked body and once again she was disgusted by the Germans. The nurse led Angila to the dressing room where she was instructed to get dressed and place the robe and slippers into a clothes bin.

An hour or so had passed and Angila realized that she had been forgotten by the staff. She opened the dressing room door and peered to her left and right. To the right, the hall led to the auditorium floor where she had last seen Talia and Dimitri. To the left, only twenty or thirty steps away, was an exit door. Angila's heart pounded as she considered making a run for it. Then reality set in. She realized that beyond that door was the Dachau Concentration Camp, which was worse than being a prisoner in this house of horrors. She had at least a chance of surviving here. More importantly, her love was here, frozen, and she might have the opportunity to revive him just as she had revived Dimitri.

She turned to her right and walked to the auditorium, which was now empty of people. She looked around the room, trying to decide where she might find Talia and Dimitri, for it was important to her to know if he was completely normal after being frozen. There was another hall on the opposite side of the auditorium floor that was in direct line with the hall she had just left. That hall led to another hall, which forced her to make a decision: left or right. She turned to her right and walked past a number of doors on either side of the hall until she heard voices in the distance. An open door to her left revealed Dimitri lying in bed, Talia lying next to him, and Hirt and his nurse standing with their backs to the open door. Talia was the first to see her standing in the doorway. Hirt turned and saw her also. He invited

Angila to join them and pointed to a metal chair where she sat. Hirt and Dimitri carried on a conversation in German for some time.

"The patient and his wife have asked if you could stay in this room for a little while. Emotional satisfaction is important to the patient's full recovery, so I have agreed to this request. You will be given one hour," Hirt said to Angila before he and his nurse left the room.

Dimitri could speak English much better than his wife, Talia, for he had been educated in the United States. He thanked Angila for her role in saving his life. "I understand that you have a husband. Do you have any questions for me?"

Angila was overcome with joy and hope for her husband when she heard his coherent conversation. "Yes. Please tell me what it was like—being frozen."

Dimitri explained that to him it was as if he had lost time. He did not remember being frozen. The last thing that he remembered was being given a shot in the arm with a needle by a nurse while he had been constrained. His next memory was of Talia's face as she was lying on top of him. "I could have been asleep for only five minutes or a week. I cannot tell the difference."

Dimitri had been frozen for a lot longer than a week. He had been frozen for a full year—the longest that anyone had ever been frozen and subsequently revived. Yet he seemed to be perfectly normal in every way. In order to test his memory, Angila asked him to tell her about his past: "How did you meet Talia, and how did you end up here?"

Dimitri was an ethnic Russian who had been born in Germany. His father worked at the Russian Embassy, as did Talia's mother. Talia's mother was Russian, but her father was German. Dimitri and Talia first met in a sandbox at the embassy's day-care center. He claimed that he loved her from the first moment he saw her. They grew up together as best friends—like a brother and sister at first, but they became lovers by the time they were in their teens. The only time they had lived apart from one another was when he had attended Harvard College in the United States, where he had earned a bachelor of science in banking and finance, and a masters in economics. His first job required him to live in Buenos Aires, Argentina, where he worked as a banker for four years. He returned to Germany at the end of the Great War—which is now referred to as World War One—and accepted a job with the Bank of Munich. He had hoped that he would be able to use his expertise to help the German economy, but it seemed that the task was too great for any one man. He reunited with Talia, and the two were married in less than a year.

Talia began to speak, but since it was in German, Dimitri had to interpret: "She wants me to tell you that I can speak five languages: German, Russian, English, French, and Spanish."

Angila replied, "Impressive," but she was far more impressed by his memory. Her thoughts turned to her husband, and she wondered how long she would have to wait until she would be able to speak to him and be held in his arms.

Dimitri, still interpreting for Talia, explained that she had learned over the past year, by overhearing the medical staff talk to one another, that Jews were not given anesthesia before being frozen and as a result, none had survived. Whispering to Angila, he said: "The rumor that Talia heard is that Hitler has a terminal disease, so this research is to determine if they can freeze him long enough to wait for science to discover a cure and then wake him up to rule over Germany once again. For this reason, they will do their best to keep your husband and me alive so that they can study us."

Angila was more hopeful than ever upon hearing this. It made sense to her. She felt as though she and her husband had a chance to survive.

Chapter 15:
The Baby Scandal

"What were Angila's duties at the Dachau Medical Research Center?"

Life for Angila improved for a time. Her primary aim at the Dachau Medical Research Center was to observe Dimitri and Talia so as to learn the best way to help her husband survive when the time came to revive him. Angila took every opportunity to ask Rascher and Hirt, "When will it be Johnny's turn?" They would not answer.

Her job as the Raschers' domestic servant was alleviated somewhat also, because the doctor was away on business for a month. He took Kamila with him, leaving Angila and Zofia to care for his wife.

Nini Rascher was a heavy drinker and a smoker. She loved the fine things that her husband provided, the expensive jewelry and furs, the servants and the huge mansion—but despite all of these things, she was not happy. On the contrary, she was a bitter woman. Fortunately for Angila, she was easier to avoid than her husband. She would often leave the house for hours at a time, not telling anyone when she would return or where she had been. Angila began to suspect that she had an illicit lover.

One night, while the doctor was away, Angila was awakened by the loud knocking of Mrs. Rascher's knuckles on Zofia's bedroom door.

"Open this door and let me in, whore!" Mrs. Rascher yelled in German.

Angila knew enough German to understand. She opened her bedroom door and saw Mrs. Rascher standing in the hall outside Zofia's room. She was wearing nothing but a sheer robe, which was untied, exposing the front side of her body. Her drink spilled from her glass to the floor as she turned to see Angila's head peering at her from down the hall. Angila quickly withdrew her head and gently closed her bedroom door, hoping to avoid being noticed by the drunken woman. There was no lock for Angila's door, and before she could return to her bed, the door flung open with such force that it struck the adjacent wall.

"Get up and make Zofia open her door," Mrs. Rascher said to Angila with a drunken slur.

Angila obeyed. She knocked gently on Zofia's door.

"Zofia dear, I think that you should open the door," Angila said in a calming tone.

Upon hearing Angila's request, Zofia opened her door. Nini Rascher pushed past the women grabbing Angila by the arm along the way. She pulled Angila inside the room with her and Zofia and slammed the door behind them. The activity caused her to spill more of her drink. This time most of the spill landed on her chest and streamed down between her breasts and stomach. The woman did not seem to care. Angila could smell the alcohol. Mrs. Rascher took another sip of alcohol.

"What belongs to my husband belongs to me. You are my husband's whores, so that makes you my whores."

She put her drink down onto the bedside table and dropped her robe to the floor. Standing there naked, she wiped her hand from her flat stomach, capturing the stream of alcohol, dragging the fluid to her breasts. Her nipples hardened as she gave Angila and Zofia a look of seduction.

Angila's legs were trembling; she was afraid of what might happen next. Suddenly, Mrs. Rascher picked up her glass from the bedside table and threw the balance of her drink into Zofia's face, likely in response to her expression of disgust.

"Who put the lock on your door? It will be removed first thing in the morning and you are never to lock your door again. Do you understand?"

Zofia replied with a nod of her head and wiped her eyes so that she could see once again. Then Mrs. Rascher demanded that Zofia undress.

"I want to see what my husband has been doing," she said.

Zofia looked at Angila with fear and uncertainty as if to ask, "What should I do?" This was a difficult situation. The sadistic Dr. Rascher might punish her for disobeying his wife, or he might disapprove of what was likely to happen next and punish her for not refusing the order.

Impatient with Zofia's delay, Mrs. Rascher shattered her drinking glass against the wall on the far side of the room and then grabbed Zofia's pajama pants and yanked them down to her ankles. The drunk woman turned to Angila: "That goes for you as well. Off with your clothes!"

Despite her reservations, Angila made the decision to obey by removing her clothes. This prompted Zofia to do the same. Mrs. Rascher crawled into Zofia's bed and commanded the girls to join her. Angila's heart sank as she moved closer to the bed. There was hardly room for the three of them in this small bed, but Mrs. Rascher insisted they join her. Zofia was lying next to Mrs. Rascher when Angila crowded onto the bed next to Zofia. The doctor's wife gave her attention first to Zofia and then to Angila: she took turns kissing their necks and fondling their breasts. Angila could smell the rank smell of cigarette smoke that lingered in the older woman's hair. Her wet tongue against her neck and breasts disgusted her, but she was more appalled by the placement of the woman's fingers.

"You are not your flesh," Zofia whispered.

The drunk woman heard the statement, which prompted her to focus her attention on Zofia once again. Angila witnessed Zofia praying, with her hands clasped together and eyes closed, while her molester's head was between her legs. Angila repeated Zofia's words: "You are not your flesh."

After several long minutes, Mrs. Rascher positioned herself between the other two women, mumbling something incoherently as she patted her twat, but seconds later she closed her eyes and her body went limp.

"Thank God!" Zofia said to Angila.

"She passed out!" Angila exclaimed.

They slowly crawled out of the bed, careful not to wake Mrs. Rascher, and sneaked out of the room.

The two of them walked quietly down the hall to the stairs, taking their time with each step so that the sound of their footsteps on the wooden treads would not interrupt her sleep. In the living quarters, the two frightened young women comforted one another. They discussed what they should do if she were to wake. They agreed to hide in separate closets.

"She will be too drunk to be able to find us, and she may not remember a thing tomorrow," Angila reasoned.

They prayed for forgiveness for their sins and thanked God for causing Mrs. Rascher to lose consciousness.

Then Zofia looked at Angila with a somber expression. "Bad news," she said.

Angila's heart sank once more. She wondered how much more bad news she could endure, but she needed to be strong for Zofia as Zofia was for her. "What is it?" she asked.

"I will have baby," Zofia replied.

Angila was stunned by the revelation. She held Zofia's hand. There was no need to ask—of course Dr. Rascher was the father.

"Does he know?" she asked.

"*Ja*, he knows," Zofia answered.

"What did he say?"

Zofia struggled to express herself in English. "He is happy. But, we not tell anyone. We say my baby is Mrs. Rascher's baby."

Angila reasoned that Mrs. Rascher must know about Zofia's pregnancy. That explained why she was hostile toward Zofia, calling her a whore. Angila thought about this terrible situation and realized that she could have gotten pregnant from the evil doctor as well. Fortunately, he hadn't been interested in her for the past several weeks, and she had had a menstrual cycle since the last rape. She gave Zofia a hug and asked her: "How do you feel about this baby?"

"You no understand, but I love my baby. His father is monster, but a child is gift from God. I no want give my baby away," Zofia explained.

"Let us pray then, for your baby," Angila said, before leading the prayer. In prayer, she asked God to protect Zofia's child from evil and to give him or her the opportunity to grow up with a kind and loving heart, free from the evil that surrounded that house, town, nation, and world.

The following day was Saturday, so Angila did not have to report to work at the Medical Research Center. She and Zofia stayed awake all night and were fully dressed in their domestic uniforms before the sun had risen. It was unnecessary however, because it was nearly noon before Mrs. Rascher wandered down the stairs from Zofia's room. Her robe was still untied, immodestly exposing her nude body. She held one hand to her head and the other on her stomach, indicating that she was suffering from a hangover. Angila was pleased that Mrs. Rascher went straight to her bedroom without saying a word to anyone. Later, the girls were also thankful that Mrs. Rascher either did not recall the events of the night before or was embarrassed by her behavior, because she never mentioned it or tried anything like that again.

Angila and Zofia were told by Mrs. Rascher the following evening to expect Dr. Rascher's and Kamila's return. They were preparing dinner when Kamila entered the kitchen with a blackened eye.

"What happened?" Angila asked, but Kamila would not answer. She would not speak at all, nor would she look the other women in the eyes. She moved methodically, as if she weren't really there. Angila surmised that something very bad had happened to her while away with Dr. Rascher. She and Zofia tried to comfort her, but Kamila seemed to be unaware of their presence.

"She is in shock," Angila said to Zofia.

That night, after everyone had gone to bed, Angila and Zofia visited Kamila in her bedroom. They encouraged her to share her experience with them so that they could properly pray for her. Kamila refused to talk about it. Whatever had happened to her while she was away with Rascher was so horrible that she could not discuss it, and it changed her for the remainder of her short life. Her spirit was broken; her faith finally shattered. Zofia ran her fingers through Kamila's long brown hair.

"My sister, we weren't there for you, but we are here for you now. Never forget, you are not your flesh," Zofia said in German, which was understood clearly by Kamila and Angila.

Kamila turned away, buried her face in her pillow, and sobbed. Never again did she laugh or smile, not even when she gave birth to her baby.

Zofia's and Kamila's babies were born within a month of one another. Both were boys who, according to Dr. Rascher, looked like him when he was a baby. Rascher named Zofia's boy Sigmund after himself, and he named Kamila's baby Adolf, in honor of you know who.

The mad Dr. Rascher publicly claimed that the boys were twins birthed by his forty-eight-year-old wife, who had previously been infertile. His explanation was that she had become pregnant as the result of taking a fertility drug that he had invented. He published a paper in prominent medical journals claiming that his new fertility drug could benefit the Third Reich by helping to produce more Aryan soldiers. This claim got Himmler's attention. He delivered a copy of a journal with Rascher's claim to Hitler. The paper included a picture of Rascher holding Zofia's baby.

Dr. Rascher was already famous in Germany for other inventions, including the widely distributed suicide pill: a cyanide capsule that could release its deadly contents with a mashing of the teeth. This gave him credibility with Hitler and as a result, Himmler received a direct order from the Fuehrer for the SS to provide a substantial research grant to the Dachau Medical Research Center. Hitler wanted to mass-produce this new miracle fertility drug so that the German people would have sufficient numbers in the future to rule the entire world.

Zofia loved her baby and cared for him as any loving mother would, but Kamila would not have anything to do with her baby, little Adolf. Mrs. Rascher had no interest in either child. Therefore Angila and Zofia fed, bathed, and comforted Kamila's baby.

Angila became Dr. Rascher's preferred sex object once Zofia and Kamila began showing their pregnancies and feared that she too would become pregnant. Fortunately, Rascher took precautions to avoid impregnating her because, she assumed, her child would be too dark to pass as an Aryan—but his insatiable sexual appetite required her to have sex with him almost every day and more than once on some days. She grew to despise the man more and more each day. After the babies were born, he became interested in Kamila and Zofia once again, leaving Angila alone for the most part. Kamila particularly resented his renewed attention.

One day, the limousine turned onto the long driveway to deliver Rascher and Angila to the mansion, as had been the routine every workday for the past year and a half, but there was unusual activity in the front of the house. Some of the male servants had placed a ladder against the front of the house to the overhanging balcony above the mansion's front door. Angila heard Fritz, the driver, say something in German to Rascher, who replied by cursing in German. That is when Angila saw the heartbreaking sight of Kamila's lifeless body hanging from the mansion's balcony. She could not take the suffering any longer.

Zofia and Angila comforted one another again that night. They prayed and talked about what motivated them to survive. For Angila, I was her motivation, as well as her Christian belief that life on this earth is temporary. Zofia said that she wanted to survive to care for her babies and explained that she wanted to care for Kamila's baby as her own.

Despite their Christian convictions, Angila expressed her concern that she might not be able to take any more heartbreak.

"My sweet, God test to see how strong. If strong faith, we spend eternity with family, and Jesus Christ."

Zofia explained that all of her family and friends had been executed or burned to death in church on that dreadful day in Lidice, but were watching over her and waiting for her to join them. "If I end my life, I spend eternity with Dr. Rascher and Adolf Hitler. We keep faith, we go when the Lord is ready. This life we forget but we forever free from evil, pain, and suffering."

This was comforting to Angila, but then she thought of Kamila. "Do you think God will punish Kamila for all of eternity for that one sin?"

"We not judge, but Bible teach we must confess, ask forgiveness, and repent. How do we do if we are dead?"

Angila did not answer, but she grappled with that question in her mind. In the end they promised one another that they would not take their own lives. Then in prayer, they made the same promise to God.

Kamila's death and the news of German setbacks in the war caused the Dr. and Mrs. Rascher to be less abusive to Angila and Zofia.

In the summer of 1943, Angila heard the news that Sicily was now in the hands of the Americans. She thought of her mother and father and of how life might have been different for her and Johnny if they had gone to Sicily, not Switzerland, from Rome. They would now be free—or would they? She suspected that Rascher's and Hirt's attitudes toward the freezing experiments had changed because they had not tried to wake anyone in over a year. Their attention seemed to focus more on perfecting poisons than anything else, and there was no research program for mass-producing an infertility pill as far as Angila could tell.

"What was your wife's relationship with the notorious Nazi, Professor August Hirt?"

Angila, worried that interest in awakening her husband had waned, asked Professor Hirt often when she could expect to see her husband. She would ask Hirt because—although he was almost as sadistic as Rascher—he seemed uninterested in sex and would answer her without using the subject as another opportunity to coerce a sexual favor from her.

"The freezing experiments have not been terminated. On the contrary, we plan to resume the awakenings, but it may be months or even another year or so before the program resumes," Professor Hirt explained.

"Another year or so?" This news was devastating to Angila. How could she carry on for another year or longer?

She saw how happy Talia and Dimitri were together and how well they were being treated. No one was raping Talia, as far as she could tell. Talia's job was to monitor Dimitri's health and report her findings each day. How happy Angila would be to report her husband's health reports.

Hirt could see the disappointment in Angila's face. He closed his office door after peering down the hall in each direction to see that no one was around to overhear their conversation. He told her to sit.

"I have a very important question to ask you. It is a very sensitive subject. One that requires the greatest levels of discretion. Can you be counted on to keep this conversation between the two of us?"

This was a different side of Hirt that Angila had never witnessed before.

"Does this have to do with my husband?"

Hirt picked up a pack a cigarettes and removed one, examining Angila's face, trying to determine if she could be trusted.

"It could have ramifications for your husband. Yes."

"I will do anything to protect my husband," she responded.

Hirt took a drag of his cigarette, paused to study Angila's facial expression once more, and decided that he should trust her. He exhaled, blowing smoke directly into her face.

"I may be able to help your husband. Maybe I can accelerate the schedule for his awakening and make your life better in the meantime, but there will be, let's say, a certain element of danger for you and for me."

Angila let him know without any uncertainty that she would do anything to achieve that goal.

Hirt took another drag of his cigarette.

"Tell me about the Rascher children."

She realized that this could be Rascher's plan to test her loyalty to him—that was how Germans operated—so she tried to buy time, hoping to verify Hirt's integrity before incriminating herself.

"What do you want to know?"

"Let me put it this way. I am in line to succeed Dr. Rascher as the executive director of the medical research center, should something happen to him. Likewise, as his number two, I might be punished if he were to do something involving this facility that displeased the SS."

"I see," said Angila.

He extinguished his cigarette, leaned back in his chair, and continued.

"As you have seen, the SS can be very harsh when administering punishment for a crime against the Reich. I have no desire to be punished for another man's crime."

"Will you confide something to me, if I confide in you?" she asked without hesitation.

"You are very brave, considering your circumstances. I admire that about you. Yes. What do you want to ask of me?"

She leaned forward and lowered her voice, aware of the potential consequence for speaking to Hirt about government affairs.

"What is the purpose of the freezing experiments and why is it taking so long to awaken my husband?'

Hirt smiled in admiration of her courage.

"If I answer this truthfully, can I count on you to keep my reply strictly confidential and to answer my questions truthfully?"

She held out her hand to shake his.

"My husband taught me that a handshake is a contract, more binding than anything written on paper."

They shook hands and then he confirmed that the rumors Talia had heard were true.

"Hitler is believed to have a terminal illness for which there is no known cure. Once the war is over, and the Allies are defeated, we will freeze Hitler in order to save him. Your husband is being tested so that we can know the best procedure for resurrecting him and what medical problems might have to be addressed upon his return. So you see, the integrity of this research program is of vital importance to the Reich, and to the Fuehrer himself."

She was satisfied that Hirt had compromised himself.

"What do you want to know about the children?"

"This institution has received a sizable grant from the military during a time of war to research the best way to mass-produce a drug that was supposedly invented here as the result of a program about which I know nothing and see no evidence of its existence. I find it remarkable that such a program could exist without my knowledge. If the grant was received by this institution as the result of fraud, I could be hanged or face an even more drastic fate, as a collaborator. On the other hand, I would receive an accommodation and promotion if I were the one to bring the crime to the attention of the authorities."

Angila recognized the opportunity. Her Christian faith taught her to love her enemies, and she tried hard to not hate all Germans, but she truly believed that all Germans were possessed by Satan—and none more so than Dr. Rascher, except maybe Hitler himself.

"Yes. I have information that may be of interest to you."

"Let's hear it, my dear," Professor Hirt said as he too leaned forward in his chair and propped his elbows on his desk.

"But first, I need you to make another promise to me," Angila said.

"I've already kept my part of the bargain. I thought a handshake is as good as a contract, yet you continue to negotiate," Hirt said, trying to mask his agitation.

"Please, one more thing. I would like assurances that I will no longer have to do things that a woman should do only with her husband. Promise that I will not have to witness any more killing or torture and that my friend Zofia and the two Rascher babies will receive the same protection."

"You have my word that I will protect you and your friend and the babies, to the best of my ability. You will live in my home as my guests. Neither of you will ever be molested or mistreated again," Hirt extended his arm to seal their contract with a handshake.

Angila and Hirt shook hands.

With those assurances, Angila told Hirt everything. He instructed her to go about her business as usual and not to say a word to anyone unless asked by gestapo agents. "Never lie to or hide anything from the gestapo," Hirt instructed.

Zofia could tell that Angila was happier than usual and inquired as to the reason for her sudden change in attitude. Angila wanted so badly to tell Zofia about her conversation with Hirt, but knew that it was best to follow his instructions. Zofia would know soon enough.

One evening around six o'clock, the gestapo paid a visit to the Rascher home. They came as three agents in plain clothes, accompanied by Hans Fischer, the SS agent whom Johnny had dubbed Scarface. The gestapo agent in charge introduced himself simply as Officer Burkhalter. He instructed Dr. Rascher to call his wife and all of his servants to gather in the main room. Hans did not acknowledge Angila, but she was the reason that he was present.

Burkhalter asked for the two Rascher babies to be brought into the room as well. Zofia and Angila complied with the order. The babies were placed in baskets on the table in the center of the room.

"What is the meaning of all of this?" Mrs. Rascher demanded to know.

"You look very fit for a woman of your age. A woman who gave birth to two children just six months ago," Burkhalter answered.

She was indignant, but Dr. Rascher's concern was evidenced by his expression.

"My husband is a famous physician and inventor—"

"Are you the mother of these children?" Burkhalter interrupted.

"Yes, these are our children. Will you please tell us what is the nature of this inquisition?" Dr. Rascher answered for his wife.

"I asked the madame the question. I would like for her to answer. Did you give birth to these children?" Burkhalter asked.

"Yes. Of course I did," Mrs. Rascher replied.

"Then you love these children as any mother would?" Burkhalter asked.

"Of course. What a stupid question," she replied with a sarcastic tone of voice.

Burkhalter suddenly withdrew a pistol from its holster and everyone in the room gasped, including the sadistic Dr. Rascher. The gestapo agent pointed the gun toward the ceiling and cocked the hammer. He lowered the gun and pointed it right at little Sigmund. Instinctively Zofia threw herself over her baby.

"No! Do not harm my baby!" Zofia screamed.

No one else had taken a step to protect the baby, including Angila who was frozen with fear and could only scream at the sight of the gun pointed at the baby. Zofia was the only one who displayed the motherly instinct to protect her child.

Burkhalter uncocked his gun, returned his pistol to its holster, and said to Mrs. Rascher who had not moved a muscle to save the baby: "I do not think that this is your baby. I don't believe you gave birth to either one of these babies."

Dr. Rascher stood suddenly to challenge the gestapo agent, but before he could mutter a word, one of the other agents punched him in the stomach, causing him to double over.

"Do you know who my husband is?" Mrs. Rascher asked.

"Yes. He is a man who is guilty of high treason in a time of war. A man who has committed fraud against the fatherland by misappropriating money. A man who is under arrest for these crimes. You are both under arrest!"

"This is a mistake. My husband—" Mrs. Rascher's protest was interrupted.

"Gather your baby. You are coming with us to answer some questions," said Hans to Zofia. Then he instructed Angila to bring the other baby.

At the Dachau headquarters, Zofia and Angila told the gestapo everything that they wanted to know about the Rascher baby scandal. As a result of their testimonies, Rascher and his wife were tried for treason and sentenced to death by hanging. They were hanged in front of the Dachau Medical Research Center, and their bodies were left hanging for three days as a warning to all that the penalty for betraying the fatherland was death.

Professor Hirt received his accommodation and promotion, just as he planned, and he kept his promises to Angila.

The girls and the two babies lived with him and his wife. They were no longer molested or humiliated. The professor and Mrs. Hirt were polite, kind, and respectful, which surprised Angila, for she knew the cruel, sadistic side of the man. He was responsible for nearly as many deaths and tortured souls as Rascher.

Zofia served as the Hirts' exclusive domestic employee. This home was much smaller and more modest than Rascher's, so the task was manageable for just one person. Unlike Rascher, Hirt paid Zofia wages for her work. She was also allowed time to care for the two boys, while Angila spent weekdays working at the Research Center. The women changed the babies' names. Zofia named her son Giovanni, in honor of Angila's husband. Kamila's baby was renamed Kam. There was one more promise to keep: my awakening.

Life was better for Angila and Zofia, but the time spent as Rascher's slaves had taken a toll on both women. Angila's beautiful hair had not had the proper attention to keep it from becoming frayed. She had not eaten properly, at times going days without eating. As a result, she was frail and malnourished.

In his role as the new executive director, Hirt ended several research programs including the most gruesome of all: the atmospheric pressure research program, also known as the pressure chamber. The center under Hirt had two primary research programs in 1944: the freezing experiments and the poison research program. The poison research program took top priority, because Hitler wanted to find more effective ways to commit mass murder.

Angila was spared the pain of having to participate in or witness the poisoning experiments, but she was aware of the program. Instead, she was allowed to work alongside Talia, monitoring the health of those who had been awakened from the deep freeze. There were currently about six such men, and another three were still frozen, awaiting their awakening. Of those frozen, I had been frozen the longest, which suggested to Angila that I was next in line to be awakened—but I had to wait.

The Dachau Medical Research Center was funded by grants from the SS, which meant that Hirt took orders from Hans Fischer, who worked for Himmler. Hans was particularly interested in me, because I had been to Argentina with his Odessa squad, the group of men assigned to smuggle

Hitler and other high-ranking Nazis to Argentina in the event that Germany were to lose the war.

Although no one dared admit it to Hitler, the D-day invasion in June of Normandy by the Allies—particularly the fact that the Americans were involved—caused a lot of high-ranking Germans, including Himmler, to fear that the end of the Third Reich was inevitable.

Things got worse in July, 1944, for the Germans. The Americans advanced in Italy as far north as Livorno and were advancing rapidly in France and elsewhere. The Soviets were advancing on the eastern front, and Hitler approved of a German withdrawal for the very first time.

As a result of these reports, Heinrich Himmler called an emergency meeting at the Dachau Medical Research Center. As Hirt's assistant, Angila was allowed to enter the room to pour water for the men. Hirt assured Himmler that Angila did not speak German, so she could not possibly understand or repeat any of the top secrets that were to be discussed. He was wrong. She and Zofia had spent the previous year teaching one another a new language. Angila learned German, and Zofia improved her English. Angila was smart enough to not allow her German captors to know about her new ability to understand them. She heard Himmler when he gave specific orders to discontinue the poison gas research program if the Allies crossed the Rhine River and place all emphasis on the freezing program. Her heart raced with excitement.

Chapter 16:
Berlin Burning

"Explain how you escaped from Dachau in April, 1945."

Lying in bed next to Angila, listening to her story about what she had lived through for the past three years made me feel terribly sad for her and guilty, for I am responsible for protecting her. She was a sheltered child before I entered her life. Instead of comforting her, as I had vowed, I had caused her to be exposed to horrible murders and sadistic brutality almost daily. Instead of being cherished, she had been the victim of sexual assault, rape, and humiliation. I wondered how she had endured the constant fear and torment, or the numerous heart-breaking events such as Kamila's suicide and Zofia having to give birth to a monster's child.

Could I have retained my sanity after enduring so much cruelty? Could anyone? I had not been a religious man. Sure, my mother and Angila made me go to Mass with them, and some things stuck—but when I realized how lucky Angila was to have had her faith, and how lucky I am that I have Angila, I closed my eyes and once again thanked God for her. She endured all of that pain, humiliation, and suffering and kept her sanity for me and for Christ.

A few days later, Professor Hirt entered the room where I was recovering and announced that Angila and I were to attend an important meeting right away.

"Get dressed quickly, and come with me," Hirt said.

We followed his instructions and allowed him to lead us to a conference room, where I met Talia and Dimitri for the first time. There were others in the room who were unfamiliar, but Zofia and the two boys, little Giovanni and Kam, were there.

"What is this? Why are you here?" Angila asked Zofia.

"I do not know. The professor brought me here and said that he would explain," Zofia answered with her much-improved English.

Hans Fischer entered the room, and Professor Hirt loudly instructed everyone in the room to "Sit down and keep quiet."

Hans stood before the room, waited until everyone was seated and paying attention to him before speaking.

"My orders are to take everyone in this room to Berlin. My orders are also to shoot anyone who tries to run away. We leave right away, so bring whatever you have with you and follow Professor Hirt to the ambulance that is waiting outside the hospital."

We followed Hirt in single file through the building to the front entrance. The moment the entrance door opened and we stepped outside of the hospital, I was surprised by the sound of explosions, sirens, airplanes, whistles, and people yelling. It was general chaos. The "hospital" must have been constructed with soundproofed walls, because I hadn't heard any of these sounds while inside. There were six ambulances lined up in a row. Hans directed Zofia and the two three-year-old boys to climb into the rear of the same ambulance that Angila and I were directed to enter. The ambulances were escorted by military jeeps, each rigged with a large-caliber machine gun mounted on the rear. I can't say for certain how many jeeps there were, but it seemed as if there were at least as many jeeps as there were ambulances. No sooner had the door been slammed shut by a soldier, than the ambulance thrust forward, causing the occupants in the rear to temporarily lose their balance. The little boys seemed to think that was some sort of game, for they laughed and wanted to do it again.

The ambulance had a small window on each side and one in the rear, allowing us to see the burning landscape as we raced from Dachau to Berlin. Angila pointed to the concentration camp that was next to the "hospital" from which we had just departed.

"Look! They are burning it to the ground," she said.

There were huge plumes of smoke rising to the clouds. We could see construction equipment in place, presumably to clean up the debris after the fire. It was a long and rough ride to Berlin. Several roads and bridges had been blown to bits, forcing the caravan to take alternative routes. In some cases, we had to leave the road altogether, driving through fields and meadows. We could hear the sound of loud canons and tanks firing. There was gunfire all around us.

We passed through all of the military checkpoints with the greatest of ease. I suppose having escorts with machine guns will do that. Berlin was under siege and was receiving the brunt of Allied bombing. Buildings of extravagant architecture had huge gaping holes, and others were on fire. Some parts of the city were unscathed, but others had impassable streets due to piles of rubble, downed trees, or overturned cars.

The convoy of ambulances came to a stop in an underground parking garage in the heart of Berlin's government district. The ambulance door to the rear was opened by a soldier. I was first to exit so that I could assist Angila, Zofia, and the boys. Along with the passengers from the other ambulances, we were led by German soldiers into the building. From there we were led down several flights of stairs to a room that must have been at least fifty feet below the street above. We were lined up with our backs to the wall facing Hans, who had two gun-wielding soldiers on either side of him. Zofia quieted the two boys. The rest of us did not need quieting. We anxiously awaited an explanation from Hans.

"As you know, each and every one of you have committed a crime that is punishable by death under German law," Hans said to us.

My heart sank. I felt as if this were the end, and I would not be able to keep my promise to Angila: to give her the life that she deserved, the house with a white picket fence, children of her own, and nothing to worry about other than what was for dinner. My first thought was to not go down without a fight. I contemplated charging one of the guards with the hope of taking his gun, but Hans lifted a sheet of paper and began to read: "I have been authorized by the Fuehrer, Adolf Hitler, to make you the following offer. These are his exact words: You were all spared in return for your participation in a valuable research program for the benefit of the fatherland. For the next few days, you will live here, in the basement of the Fuehrer's bunker. When I, Adolph

Hitler, the Fuehrer of the Third Reich, instruct you to do so, you will all leave this room together and relocate to my new headquarters. This process may give some of you the idea to attempt to escape. If you make this attempt you will be shot, and your families will be punished. If you cooperate, you will gain your life, your freedom, and ten ounces of gold, once we have concluded our study of the freezing effects, which will be no longer than one year from today. In the meantime, you will be cared for in the most respectful manner. Food, drink, and cots will be delivered to this room shortly."

Angila explained to me that all of the other men who were present had been frozen also. We were all perplexed as to why Zofia and the children were included in this group. I wondered what benefit they could be to Hitler.

Hans left the room, but the armed guards remained. A short time later, the doors opened and several young blond girls—presumably Germans—entered the room to set up tables and chairs. Their next task was to bring food and pitchers of beer for the adults and milk for the two boys. We took our places at the tables and enjoyed a delicious hot meal. The blondes brought cots and blankets and arranged them neatly on the floor while we enjoyed our dinner.

Each cot was big enough for a small woman or a child, but not quite long enough for an average man. My feet hung off the end and onto the concrete floor, unless I lay on my side and bent my knees. We arranged our cots so that Angila was next to me, and the two boys were between her and Zofia. The boys were full of energy, so we allowed them to run around the room so that they would be easier to put to bed. There was hardly anything they could hurt in this place. The floor, walls, and ceiling were all barren concrete. There were no pictures—not even of Hitler—and no windows or decorations of any kind. It's easy to lose track of time in such a place.

The third and final day that we were there, the door was flung open and in walked Hans with six armed guards. The guards held their machine guns, not pointing at us but ready just in case. Behind them came an attractive blonde and Adolf Hitler! This came as a complete surprise to us, as we had no warning. Everyone in the room began to spring to their feet, but Hans was quick to tell everyone to "remain as you were."

Hitler and the blonde sat in chairs at one of the tables where we ate our meals. Hitler looked defeated. He did not make eye contact with any of us, and his posture was not that of a confident man.

Suddenly, more men entered the room. Two decorated military men, likely generals, and a blonde, and Adolf Hitler! But Hitler was already in the room, sitting in the chair. I did a double take. There were two Hitlers and two blondes. Of all the people in the room, I should have been surprised the least, being a double myself. It was apparent that the second Hitler was the real thing. He exuded confidence and looked as though he was filled with hate and contempt.

Once again Hans instructed us to remain seated. The timid Hitler and the blonde seated next to him stood up as the real Hitler approached them. Zofia translated the conversation.

"The time has come. You know what to do. You will be remembered for your contribution to the fatherland and your families will be cared for. Are you ready to make the ultimate sacrifice for your Fuehrer?" Hitler said to the doubles.

The timid Hitler and the blonde next to him acknowledged that they were ready and willing. With that, the impostors left the room with the entourage that had accompanied the real Hitler, and the real Adolf Hitler and his new bride, Eva, remained with our group. Hitler surveyed the crowd, looking over each one of us. His eyes were dark and his hands were shaking. His head and legs were shaking too. He looked exhausted and meandered around the room as if senile. Hitler's wife, Eva, was surprisingly attractive. I could not help but notice her shapely legs. Angila could not help but notice me noticing.

"The time has come. We are going to leave this room together and escort the Fuehrer to a plane that is waiting to take all of us to a secret location outside of Germany. As you can see, this mission is vital to the fatherland and to the building of the Fourth Reich. We will not tolerate anything less than strict obedience and discipline. Now, follow me," Hans announced.

Hans led the way with two armed soldiers walking on either side of Adolph and Eva Hitler. Two soldiers walked in front of the rest of the group, while two followed in the rear. There were others involved with helping us make our getaway. It was a well-planned mission. We entered the garage and once again took our places in the ambulances. We were instructed by the driver to keep our heads down. I complied for the most part but could not resist peering out the window on occasion. I recall seeing a clock tower; the hands indicated that it was shortly after midnight.

The city of Berlin was on fire. Despite the explosions, we made our way to the boulevard at the Hohenzollerndamm, which ran through the center of Berlin. A Junkers Ju 52 transport aircraft awaited us. We quickly crowded onto the plane. The wide boulevard was empty of automobiles, which allowed the plane to use it as a runway.

The plane took off. I expected the plane would draw fire, but we were able to depart without being noticed by the Allies, who were already within Berlin city limits.

I looked at Angila and she looked at me while we held hands.

"I do not know what fate God has planned for us, but I am happy that we are together," she said.

I kissed her, and told her that I felt the same. Quite frankly, I was tired. I had had enough adventure in my life.

"When we get to wherever we are going, we are going to make a run for it the first chance we get and we are going to have the most boring life together for the rest of our life," I whispered to her.

"That sounds nice," she said, smiling.

Then she placed her head on my shoulder. I leaned my head onto hers. We fell asleep but were awakened a few hours later when we landed in Denmark to refuel. It would be hours before sunrise, so we fell asleep once more. The wheels touched down again, this time on a runway in Spain, waking us once again. The sun was shining, so we were awake for the day. Thankfully, the three-year-old was sound asleep next to Zofia. Soon the plane was in the air once more. We were over the Atlantic for quite some time before landing for the last time. This time we were on one of the Canary Islands.

Hans instructed everyone to exit the plane in an orderly fashion. Hitler was wearing a disguise. Most noticeably, his funny Charlie Chaplin mustache was gone. There was a line of cars waiting to take us from the airport to the harbor. Once there, our driver opened our doors and told us in English to take our places with the others who were in line on the dock.

The sun was high in the sky, indicating that it was around noon. We took our place with the others on the dock. There were two submarines, one on either side of the dock. Men were working to remove the swastika from one of the subs. The swastika had already been removed from the other.

Hitler and Eva got onto the submarine without the swastika. The rest of us, including Hans, Professor Hirt, Talia and Dimitri, Zofia and the boys, and Angila and me, were instructed to get on board the other submarine. Hans was clearly in charge. He commanded us to take to our bunks, and he showed each one of us where that was.

The submarine left port and quickly submerged. The bunk bed was more comfortable than the cot from the previous night, but it certainly wasn't the bed from our home in Paris. Angila's bunk was above mine, but we both crowded into my bunk. Her body felt so good next to mine.

"I wonder where we are going," she said.

"Argentina," I replied without hesitation.

"What is in store for us?" Angila asked.

"I'm certain that they want to continue to study my health, to see what, if any, side effects may occur as a result of freezing me—but I assure you that I will find a way for you and I to escape and to return to our home on the beach in Panama," I promised. I sealed my promise with a kiss.

"That sounds wonderful. I will appreciate Panama even more than before."

Lying there with her head on my chest, my arm wrapped around her, my mind began to whirl. I tried to focus on a plan of escape. I tried to remember as much as I could about Argentina—the various safe houses and the surrounding towns, but my mind wandered. I recalled once again what Angila told me about: the terrible murders, the torturous experiments, the rapes, the suicide of her friend, and seeing her husband frozen in a block of ice. Then I thought about the terrible things that I witnessed. The most gruesome thing that continued to stick out in my mind was the pained expression on the face of the man in the pressure chamber just before he exploded, but the most emotional thing that I recalled was the massacre at Lidice. The pain on the faces of the women and children as they were forced to see their husbands, sons, and fathers executed for simply being a resident of the same town as a rebel fighter who killed a Nazi general. Once again, I wondered how Angila could believe that there is a loving God, when we had witnessed so much evil.

Deep below the ocean's surface my thoughts turned to the soldiers on board the submarine. What sort of men would continue to follow a madman who was responsible for the total destruction of their nation? Could these soldiers not see that Hitler was evil and that everyone he touched suffered or died? What supernatural powers did Hitler possess that could cause people to follow him, especially after his obvious defeat? Was Hitler really Satan?

I tried to force myself to stop pondering philosophical questions and focus on an escape plan, but my mind continued to wander. I began to daydream about a happy life with Angila, far, far away from evil—away from Nazis, war, and the Mafia. I remembered how enjoyable our life was during the short time that we lived in our beach house in Panama. I thought of the walks on the beach at sunset and waking up in the morning to the sound of waves crashing onto the sand. I smiled when I recalled trying to make love to Angila in our hammock, only to flip and land flat on our backs in the sand. Then, I remembered that I had a small fortune in a Panamanian bank! When Angila had convinced me to move her from Panama to New Orleans, I had left several hundred thousand dollars behind as a nest egg. We must find a way to return to Panama.

I felt as if this were the end of an unhappy chapter in our lives, and that happiness was just around the corner.

Chapter 17:
Return to Argentina

"You testified in your deposition that you arrived in Argentina with Adolf Hitler on May 18, 1945. Describe to the court what happened."

The intercom speakers blared an alarm throughout the submarine gaining everyone's attention. We formed a straight line as instructed, and followed Hans up the ladder to the submarine's deck. The moon and stars provided the only light, but we could see that the other submarine had also surfaced with its occupants gathered on deck. The German submariners inflated rubber lifeboats, which we used to get to shore. We disembarked around 11:00 p.m. near the small port of Necochea, about three hundred miles south of Buenos Aires.

An assemblage of about one hundred people, mostly men, were gathered on the shore. There were four men with pack mules waiting to greet us. Hitler and his wife rode in a wagon drawn by two of the mules. The other mules were loaded with provisions and pulled another wagon carrying a large, heavy trunk, which had taken four men to lift. The rest of us walked. Three hours later we stopped to make camp. Despite our predicament, it was a pleasant night to sleep under the stars.

With the morning sun, I could see that we had followed a beautiful river that divided a grassy plain. It seemed so peaceful. Hitler appeared to me as a small figure among the huge, empty expanse of green. I feared him less and had more hope of being able to free ourselves from our captors.

We were served breakfast by campfire and waited until midmorning for a convoy of trucks to arrive. They could be seen coming from far away, because of the dust cloud they created over the open prairie.

The flatbeds of the trucks were covered with straw and hay, which helped soften the ride, but it was still a very uncomfortable and long drive to San Carlos de Barilche. The trucks came to a stop just outside of the town. Hitler, Hans, and a few other men assembled, likely discussing the next move. From there, the group divided into smaller groups and we descended upon the town. Hans led our group consisting of Zofia, the boys, Dimitri and Talia, Angila and me to a rancher's private residence, where we all gathered in his stable. We were fed and Hans instructed us to rest.

"We still have a journey ahead of us," said Hans.

Why did you not try to escape when you, Dimitri, and the others outnumbered Hans?

I peered through the window at the outside world, hoping to see which way we should go if were to attempt an escape. I saw German soldiers setting up a ring of tents. We were completely surrounded by enemy guards. Dimitri observed me and guessed what I was thinking.

"There are several of us and only one Hans," Dimitri whispered into my ear.

"Hans isn't our only concern." I pointed to the tents in the distance.

Dimitri peered through the glass and understood. "I see."

Dimitri was much younger and despite having been frozen for months his muscles seemed to all but split his skin open. He appeared to be as strong as an ox and as tough as a nail. It would be comforting to have him as an ally if we had to resort to using brute force to gain our freedom.

"This is not the time, but when the opportunity arises, can I count on you?"

"Yes, you certainly may. We must be free of these villains," he replied.

The following morning we gathered in the open air outside the stable. Hitler, Hirt, and company were noticeably absent. A rancher provided us with horses and mules to make the long, uphill journey into the Andes Mountains. Counting the boys, Giovanni and Kam, there were sixteen in our group.

Neither Angila nor I had ever ridden a horse before, and the trail was very treacherous. Thankfully, we needed only to hold on tightly to the horses, for the horses knew this path well. For additional safety, Hans tied Angila's horse to his, mine to hers, and so on. Zofia and the two boys rode in a horse-drawn wagon.

The first part of the highway was wide enough for two trucks to pass one another going in opposite directions, but we came upon a section that was blocked by fallen rocks. Hans said that he knew of an alternative route, but it would be more dangerous and too narrow for the wagon. The two boys, Kam and Giovanni, would have to ride double with someone. Dimitri and I volunteered, but considering our lack of equestrian experience, Hans elected to have the boys ride with guards who had served in the German cavalry. Zofia rode horseback with a third soldier.

The alternative route was a trail that narrowed to less than twelve inches in some places. It was a harrowing experience. Rising above us to our left was a sheer wall of rock that seemed to be leaning in our direction as if were about to topple onto us. To our right was a long, rock-filled drop to the canyon floor.

My horse's foot slipped on several occasions causing rocks to slide off into the abyss below.

"Do not look down!" Hans yelled.

I was glad that Angila was before me so that I could keep an eye on her. Not that I could do anything to help her if she ran into trouble, but it kept me from turning around to look for her—which Hans also warned against.

"It is important to look forward at all times. Otherwise you may lose your balance," Hans instructed.

He didn't have to tell me twice. The winding trail led us up higher and higher, and the air seemed colder with every step. We had been provided with parkas and gloves, but we weren't wearing them. I worried about the boys. They were surely cold. After some time we came to a place where the trail had fallen away, leaving a four-foot gap for the horses to jump. The trail rose before us more steeply than before, so I could see the first horse, carrying a solo guard, complete the jump across the gap. I nervously watched as the rider bounced a bit as the horse landed, but he survived the leap without incident. The second rider did the same. Next it was the horse carrying Kam and a soldier. The muscles in my neck and back stiffened with nervousness, and I imagined how nervous Zofia and Angila must have been at that moment. They hopped across the crevasse without incident. I exhaled the breath that I had been holding. Then little Giovanni and his soldier jumped across the crevasse with their horse. I felt another sigh of relief when both of the boys were across the gap.

Zofia and her guard followed, but their horse did not clear the gap cleanly. I suppose due to the weight of two adults the horse misjudged the jump, slipped, and lost its footing. I bristled at the sound of Zofia's scream as one leg slipped off the ledge causing the horse and riders to shift. Angila screamed as well. The horseman used his skill to regain their balance and the horse's footing, and they made it across safely—but their disruption caused a problem for the rider behind them. The solo soldier's horse had already begun to jump when the horse carrying Zofia stalled. The soldier attempted to pull back, but his horse's momentum caused them both to fall off the cliff, and with a horrific scream, he and his horse tumbled off the side of the mountain into the abyss far below. I remembered that my horse was tied to Angila's, and hers was tied to Hans's horse. My heart pounded with fear because I worried that this frightening sight might cause panic among the horses and set off a dreadful chain reaction. I had to convince myself to remain calm and was thankful that no one panicked.

Hans yelled a reminder to not look back.

The rest of us made it across the crevasse without incident, but I wondered how much more treacherous the trail might be ahead. There was no choice but to forge ahead, because there was not enough room on the narrow trail for a horse to turn around. I wondered what would happen if we met an approaching envoy on horseback. My worries were for naught, because that was the worst of the trail.

Soon we returned to the highway. I felt a huge sense of relief upon gaining plenty of distance from the cliff. Despite having donned our coats, hats, gloves, and earmuffs, the next problems that we encountered were the cold and snow. I was reminded of the bitter cold that I felt upon my awakening and shivered at the thought. We had traveled higher and higher in elevation and now were in the snowcap, which remained frozen all year round. The highway could hardly be seen, for it was covered with snow and ice, but we could see our destination. It looked like a castle from a distance, but as we approached the huge concrete structure looked more like a military fort. Suddenly, I recognized where we were. This was where I had purchased the land for Professor Hirt and Hans when I was in Argentina years ago. I also recalled that there was a better route to this place than the way we had come, for we had driven an automobile all the way to the property. There must be a reason why Hans had brought us this way and not the safer and easier route.

The compound was built in part on a huge natural ledge, with the balance being inside the mountain. Dynamite had obviously been used to blast away huge chunks of rock and granite. The exterior concrete walls of the compound rose twenty feet or more. Armed guards dressed in civilian clothes opened the steel gates to allow for our entry. They appeared to be German, but I did not hear them speak.

Once inside and the doors closed behind us, Hans instructed us to dismount and arrange ourselves in a line facing him. We were in an open courtyard surrounded by a complex of connected buildings that reminded me of a medieval village with modern construction. To my right was a four-story structure with few windows, which seemed to melt away into the mountain. Straight ahead, past Hans who was facing our group, was a well-camouflaged tower that could not be distinguished from the mountain from a distance. Atop the tower was a tall antenna. At the courtyard level, there was an opening large enough for the largest truck to pass—not that I expected to see a truck way up there.

The soldiers took the horses away to a stable on the perimeter of the compound. A tall, thin man dressed in civilian clothes approached Hans. He had a square face and a noticeably strong chin. He exchanged words with Hans and then, with a heavy German accent, introduced himself.

"Welcome to your new home, we've named it Berchtesgaden, also called the Berghof in honor of *der Fuehrer's* favorite vacation home. My name is Karl Van der Kamp, and I am the Berghof director. We wish for you to feel at home here, as part of our family. From here, we will build the Fourth Reich, and would like for you to be a part of our glorious history. Follow me and I will show you around," said Van der Kamp.

His words were comforting—not because I trusted him, but because I surmised that security was lax, hence the reason for wanting us to feel welcome. I was wrong.

Van der Kamp led us to the far side of the courtyard, to the left of the tower and opposite the four-story building.

"This is the administration building which provides services for operating the Berghof," Van der Kamp explained. He opened the door and led us to the cafeteria. We were glad to get out of the cold.

"This is where the entire community dines. You will be given specific times for your meals. I caution you not to miss your allocated mealtime, for you will not be allowed in at any other hour."

Van der Kamp led us back to the courtyard and continued the tour. The compound's courtyard was generally circular. We crossed the courtyard to tour the four-story building.

"This is your apartment building, we call it *der Himmel*, or in English, Heaven," said Van der Kamp.

Angila and I looked at one another simultaneously with the same expression of skepticism. Van der Kamp showed us the apartment amenities: a heated pool, gymnasium, and a recreation center complete with indoor tennis. Next to *der Himmel* was a medical building, equipped with the most advanced technology of the day.

We weren't shown all of the compound, particularly the section that gave the place its purpose, until weeks later. At the conclusion of the tour, Van der Kamp took each of us to our individual apartment, which was no more than a single room, but Angila and I were pleased to see that it came with a private bathroom. The room was small and windowless. The bed was very comfortable compared to every bed that we had slept in since we left our home in Paris. A thorough inspection of our room did not reveal any hidden listening devices, but as a precaution, we spoke to one another in Italian.

Zofia and her boys were in the room directly across the hall from our room. She told us that she had decided to raise Kam as her own. I was relieved to hear this because I was worried that Angila might want to adopt the boy. Angila wanted a child of her own, and I planned to provide that for her, but I was forty-five and not getting any younger. This added to my motivation to escape with Angila. We longed for the home with the white picket fence, filled with children laughing and playing. But for the moment, we were preoccupied with staying alive first, and obtaining freedom second. Besides, even though Kam was not responsible for his father's sins, he would serve as a permanent reminder of the satanic demon and all of the time that I intended to forget once we were safely behind the white picket fence.

Zofia became Kam's mother, but Angila and Talia helped care for both of the boys. I saw Angila's motherly nurturing skills for the first time. She was a natural. She could remain calm when the boys were in the throes of a temper tantrum. She was gentle and loving but communicated with them about proper behavior in a way that they understood. It was important to Angila and Zophia to teach the boys to follow Jesus, so she and Zofia took turns singing Christian songs to them at night, after having read them Bible stories.

While the women cared for the children, Dimitri and I tried to develop an escape plan. We spent the first days walking, talking, surveying, and planning. One day, Professor Hirt ordered Dimitri and me to meet him at the medical station, where we were examined. He examined our heart and lung functions and other vital signs, and indicated that he was very pleased with his observation. As we were returning to *der Himmel,* Dimitri and I talked about the lives that we wanted. Our goals were surprisingly similar.

"I don't know why I keep imagining a home with a porch swing and a yard with a white picket fence, but as silly as it sounds, those are the symbols of peace and serenity for me. Maybe it's because I remember all of the similar homes that lined St. Charles Street in uptown New Orleans. As a child I dreamed of being rich enough to live there, and I made it. Angila and I lived in a beautiful antebellum home right there in the Garden District," I said.

"There is nothing silly about this, my friend. I dream of the day when Talia and I will have boys that I can teach to play football. You did not know that I was on the football team in my school. But—and don't laugh—but I wish to become a gourmet chef," said Dimitri.

I didn't laugh; in fact I told him that I thought his goals were admirable. I also told him about my beach house and bank account in Panama.

"If we help one another to escape this place, I have enough money to buy a restaurant. We will be partners—you can run the restaurant and I will run the bar and maybe even a little gambling house on top." My days as a mobster influenced that idea, then suddenly I realized that I wanted nothing to do with that life any longer.

"Forget that last part, no gambling. I can loan you money to build a beach house next to mine. You can pay me as you can from profits from our business," I said with enthusiasm. It felt good to think of better times ahead.

Dimitri said that he loved the plan. We shook hands as partners and spent the next few weeks trying, with greater determination, to glean as much information as possible so that we could devise an escape plan. Dimitri was invaluable due to his ability to speak German and Spanish. Our captors spoke German and English, so Dmitri and I talked to one another in Spanish when we didn't want to risk being overheard by one of the Nazis. Our women, including Zofia, also served as our spies, for I was the only one in our group who did not speak or understand German.

Through our collective efforts, we determined that Hitler and his closest followers, including Professor Hirt, were living in the valley at the foot of the mountain at a place called the Hacienda San Ramón. Tens of thousands of Germans were in Argentina, ready to overthrow the Argentinean government and install Hitler as supreme dictator of the Fourth Reich. All across Argentina, Germans posed as ordinary citizens, awaiting their orders to leap into action, but the Berghof was the epicenter of their organization. We learned that the tower was much more extensive than the part that could be seen from the courtyard and served as the Nazis' command and control center. It also housed the electrical substation and more importantly it housed the remains of the German national treasury. I imagined gold and silver looted days before the Allies entered Berlin.

"The big problem for the Nazis is that Hitler is sick," Dimitri explained.

"How do you think that will affect the Nazi plan for overthrowing the Argentinean government? More importantly, what do you think that means for us?" I asked.

"A meeting is being held at the Hacienda this very moment to decide the answers to those questions. I suppose that if Hitler were to suddenly die or was too sick to proceed, their entire plan would be scrapped, and that would be the end of their hopes for a Fourth Reich," Dimitri replied.

"Do we know their options?" I asked.

"Talia overheard German scientists discussing a new discipline called cryogenics. She is convinced that they plan to freeze Hitler and use the gold from the treasury to fund cancer research, with the hope of resurrecting him once a cure is found. No one knows how long that will be—five years? Ten?"

"Why are they keeping us here? And what use are the children, little Giovanni and Kam, to them?"

"That, my friend, is the bad news. They plan to freeze ten people that they deem expendable, so that when the time comes to thaw Hitler, they can practice on us first," Dimitri answered.

This was terrible news. The thought of being refrozen and leaving Angila vulnerable again was intolerable.

"Dimitri, we are running out of time. We must make an escape as soon as possible," I said frantically.

"But how? This place is a fortress, and even if we could walk out that door, it is a long, long way to civilization. If we don't freeze to death, they would surely catch us before we were a kilometer away from here," he said.

"I don't know, but we need to think of something fast."

I felt a sudden rush of anxiety. I was determined to get Angila and the others to safety, so that we could have a normal life and raise children in a home with that white picket fence. She was depending on me to find a way, but at that moment, I felt a sense of hopelessness. In desperation, I asked a question that I already knew the answer to.

"Suppose we kill Hitler?"

Dimitri could tell that I was distraught and was desperate for a solution. He put his hand on my shoulder.

"My friend, I want to take my wife away from these evil people once and for all as much as you do. I want to be your business partner. Can you see me wearing that silly hat?" he said with a comforting smile.

I felt ashamed that this much younger man was reassuring me, instead of the other way around.

"But you know that these people would torture and kill us in the worst possible way, and considering their experience with torture and killing, I don't want to chance it—unless we find out that they plan to kill us anyway. In that case I say that we rush one of the guards, take his gun, and kill as many of the bastards as possible," he continued.

"Yes, I suppose that you are right."

We shook hands, and agreed to sneak out of our rooms two hours past midnight to explore possible escape routes.

Angila and I made love that night as if it were the last night of our lives. She was asleep well before midnight, but my mind was preoccupied with planning my response to the various scenarios that could present themselves if we were caught trying to escape. I thought about where we should go and what we should do if we managed to make it down the steep, treacherous mountain. Professor Hirt had given Angila a cheap watch, likely pilfered from one of the Jews from the Dachau Concentration Camp, which she had placed on the bedside table. It was two o'clock, the time that I had agreed to meet Dimitri. I eased out of bed, careful not to wake my sweetheart, and quietly crossed the room to gather my clothes. I took the parka that was provided to me for our inbound journey to the Berghof. I dressed quickly but quietly.

Dimitri was waiting for me in the hall outside our rooms. Without saying a word, he walked to the end of the curved hall to a heavy metal door that led to the staircase. We paused before opening the door, uncertain if we might set off an alarm alerting the guards to our presence. Dimitri pushed the crossbar down, releasing the door latch. The heavy latch made a loud noise that reverberated down the hall, but we did not hear an alarm. There were two sets of stairs, one set for going up, the other for going down. We chose first to go down one flight and investigate. Peering through the door's glass window, we could see that this floor looked identical to the one above, so we went down one more flight of stairs. This level provided us with more options. We could go through a door which led to yet another hall that looked identical to the ones that we had just seen, or we could go through an exit door which opened to the outside world.

Again, we were concerned about setting off an alarm, but to our surprise, this door opened without incident. The door was designed to lock automatically upon closing, so I removed one of my gloves and used it to keep the door from closing all the way. It was blistering cold, well below zero. I could feel the moisture in my eyes beginning to freeze. It was so dark, we could hardly see our hands just a few inches before our face.

"Imagine trying to sneak two toddlers and three women out of here in these conditions, and don't forget about that huge crevasse on the narrow trail that we would have to leap over while carrying children," Dimitri said.

He was right. We were unfamiliar with the trail—but the horses weren't.

"Dimitri, where are the horses that brought us here?" I asked.

"I don't know. I haven't seen them since they were stowed away in the stable the day that we arrived."

"The horses know the way, even in the dark, and can jump over the gap, even carrying children," I said with desperate hope.

"True, but how are we going to sneak horses through the building to where we are now, even if we can find them?" Dimitri asked.

Dimitri was too pragmatic, always thinking of why things wouldn't work.

"First things first. We must locate the horses tomorrow," I responded.

Dimitri placated me by agreeing, because he felt that my idea of escaping was doomed before it started. He was right.

The following morning, the alarm on Angila's watch alerted us that it was six o'clock. We wouldn't have known otherwise, because the windowless room gave no clues to the outside world. Angila was lying next to me. Her eyes were open wide, staring at the ceiling, apparently in deep thought.

We exchanged good morning hugs, kisses, and greetings, and then I told her about our plan to locate the horses.

Angila expressed her concern about the dangers of trying to escape.

"My darling, suppose we were to make it all the way down the mountain safely, where would we go? We will have to pass the Hacienda where Hitler, Hirt, and other Nazis live, and the nearest town is filled with Nazis. Then what? We don't know our way around Argentina," she argued.

"Yes dear, we do. Dimitri and I have been here before. He lived in Argentina for a few years, and I was involved in the purchase of this property as well as the Hacienda. Our first challenge is getting the horses out of this compound unnoticed. The next challenge is getting down the mountain. From there, I can get us to safety. We must try. Otherwise, they plan to freeze Dimitri and me. I can't leave you alone, unprotected, with these monsters again," I said.

"Johnny?"

"Yes?"

"Would it be so terrible if they froze both of us, and we woke up together in a few years from now to a better world?'

I could not believe my ears. She sounded as if she had surrendered.

"Angila, that is crazy talk. Why would you ask such a question?"

She turned to face me, running her fingers through my hair.

"This life has not been good to us. I'm tired, and I am ready to sleep for a long time and wake up to a new life," she said.

"Sweetheart, please don't give up. We can't let them freeze us. It's too dangerous."

"More dangerous than traveling down a steep mountain in subzero temperatures with people chasing us and other people waiting at the end of the trail to catch us?"

Her reply reminded me of Dimitri's logic. "Yes, letting them freeze us is more dangerous. At least if we run we have a chance. If they freeze us, how do we know how long it will be before they awaken us? They might not ever find a cure for Hitler's cancer and even if they do, no one knows the long-term effects of freezing, or how long is too long to freeze someone," I argued.

"But if we die, we will be together in heaven. Johnny, we are in hell, and I'm ready for heaven."

"We are going to make it. You must not lose faith," I pleaded.

I had to think of something to encourage her to forget the idea of surrendering.

"Speaking of faith, if they freeze us, and we are still alive, wouldn't our souls be trapped in our frozen bodies, keeping us from reaching heaven?" I said, hoping to appeal to her Christian faith.

She thought about that point, and I was proud of myself for thinking of it.

"When the Lord is ready for us, our souls will be in heaven. If we are frozen, we will be together and it will be painless. If we survive and are awakened, that will mean that God has a plan for us in the future. If he is ready for us before that, we will be called to his side," she replied.

"Ah, but wouldn't the same principal apply if we try to escape? If he has a plan for us in the future, we will escape, but if he is ready for us, we will be killed anyway. So, I say that we try to make it. Let's get out of here and go back to our beach house in Panama," I said proudly, thinking that I had won the argument convincingly.

"I will love you until the end of time," was her reply, and then she climbed on top of me and made love to me once more. That shut me up.

Dimitri and I were on our way to the gymnasium later that morning to participate in our routine program, where our captors would monitor our vital signs as we exercised. Hans approached.

"We have a change in your program today. Follow me," he said.

My first thought was that he must have learned of our leaving the building last night. Hans led the way through the tower's tunnel and then down a flight of stairs where there were two rows of heavily armed guards, eight in total, wearing SS uniforms, on either side of the stairs. Dimitri and I looked at each other with concern.

"I hope to God that this isn't it. I cannot let them freeze me without telling Angila goodbye," I said to Dimitri.

"I agree, my friend. I hope this is not the end either, but I have a bad feeling," Dimitri replied.

We were led down ten flights of stairs, to far below the courtyard level. The compound was far more enormous than I had imagined. There were more guards, but these were wearing SS uniforms and holding machine guns. My heart pounded so hard that I could feel my pulse in my fingertips. I felt helpless and uncertain what to do. Hans led us into a conference room where three men were already seated.

"These men were frozen in Dachau, like you and me. I recognize many of them," Dimitri whispered.

"This is it then. I knew it. We are going to have to overcome a couple of guards and shoot our way out," I replied. I kept seeing the image of Angila and me splashing in the surf in front of our beach house. Behind the white picket fence I could see a little boy and a little girl playing on the porch swing.

Professor Hirt and Director Van der Kamp were standing in front of the room as if to give a presentation to their seated audience. Dimitri and I took our seats. Five chairs remained empty.

"I thought that you said they were going to freeze ten expendables? There are only five of us in this room," I said to Dimitri.

Hans interrupted our conversation before Dimitri could reply.

"Many of you know by now your purpose for being here. Each and every one of you are guilty of committing crimes against the Third Reich and were facing the death penalty, but were spared in return for your participation in a valuable research program for the benefit of the fatherland. You were told that if you cooperated, you would regain your freedom once we have concluded our freezing experiments. The time is near for you to be free once again. Each of you will find, underneath your chair, a bag containing ten ounces of gold coins. This is yours to bring with you when we leave this room," said Hans.

"It has been my pleasure to have you as my guest. I will miss seeing you after today," said Van der Kamp.

I thought: what a sick bastard; treating us as if we had volunteered to be here.

"You deserve to know what is expected of you from this moment forward," said Professor Hirt.

Hirt turned and drew open a green curtain on the wall behind him, which revealed a large pane glass window. On the other side was a huge warehouse. The room was lit by bright industrial lights that were obscured from view. The walls were either painted black or they were far off in the distance, because they could not be seen. There were rows of large Nazi banners hanging from the ceiling. The focal point of the room was something that I couldn't make out. It was straight ahead at the farthest point from our room.

"By now you all know that the fatherland is occupied by our enemies, the Russians, Americans, British, and the rest of the countries run by Jews—the so-called Allies," said Hirt.

Hans opened the door. Van der Kamp exited the room first.

"Follow me as I talk," Hirt said as he followed Van der Kamp.

The five of us stood up and followed Hirt out the door and to a door leading to the room on the other side of the glass pane window. Hans closed the door and followed behind. There was a coatrack filled with parkas. We were instructed to put them on. Mine was too big, but that didn't matter. A pair of gloves was in one of the coat pockets. The parka and gloves were useful because it was really cold in this room; maybe a hundred and fifty below zero.

There were stacks of something that looked like coffins, and there must have been a hundred uniformed German soldiers standing guard with machine guns. Hirt would take a few steps then turn to us to speak, then turn and repeat the process.

"Fate gave the enemies of the Third Reich an opportunity: our glorious leader, Adolf Hitler, was stricken by a potentially fatal disease, one without a current cure and which affected his mastermind. As a result, mistakes were made that cost us the battle of the fatherland, but the war is not over. Nazi Germany shall never be defeated!"

By now, we were at the focal point of the room: a glass coffin with someone inside. I noticed that several of the armed guards moved closer as if ready to spring into action if necessary. Hirt stepped onto a platform and instructed us to do the same, where we could see that the man in the coffin was Adolf Hitler. He was frozen.

Hirt waved his arms in the air to the left and then the right, pointing to rows and rows of stacked coffins, each bearing a red swastika. "Behold ten thousand of *der Fuehrer's* most loyal and best trained soldiers."

"Holy crap!" I said instinctively before turning to Dimitri. "How could this many people be willing to be frozen for a man who led their country to total destruction?" I asked.

"A well planned schedule is in place for the awakening of a certain number of these soldiers periodically until it is time for awakening *der Fuehrer*. At that time, all of the soldiers will be awakened!"

"Then what do you need us for?" I asked. Everyone's head turned in my direction.

"Herr Cado. Before we wake soldiers, we will wake a test patient to ensure that the current technique that is being employed at that time has been perfected," Hirt replied.

"How often are these intervals? I mean, how long do you think it will be before Hitler is awakened?" I asked.

"The intervals may vary, depending on the circumstances, but I think annual awakenings will be common. We are hopeful that we will awaken everybody in four or five years, but no more than ten years. That is why we picked ten of you," Hirt answered.

The five of us looked around and counted one another.

"But there are only five of us," Dimitri stated.

Hans stepped onto the platform and handed some envelopes to Hirt, who then passed one to each of the five of us. My heart sank when I opened mine, for it was a letter from Angila. My eyes filled with tears, making it difficult to read.

"Read the letter from your wife to the court."

My dearest Giovanni,

You are the love of my life and I love you and will always love you until death do us part. Please forgive me for not telling you that I made a contract with Professor Hirt where he would protect us to the best of his abilities. He arranged this contract between Adolf Hitler and you and me. I prayed about this, Johnny, and I believe this is our one way to be together. I am waiting for you, please join me.

With all my heart and love,

Your Angila

The letter was accompanied by a contract that was in German, so I asked Dimitri to read it. He was crying. He had a similar letter from Talia. I looked around, and the other three had letters.

"What does the contract say? Please tell me," I pleaded.

Dimitri wiped the tears from his eyes and read: "By order of Adolf Hitler, all German people must obey for all time the terms of this contract. Then it says that we are to be awakened no later than the day of his awakening, but may be awakened any time prior to that day. Every effort must be used to preserve our good health, and upon our awakening we will be free of all future commitments to the German Reich, the Nazi Party and Adolf Hitler. We are to be guaranteed safe travel and the right to keep our ten ounces of gold. There's more, but those are the main points."

"Where is Angila?" I demanded of Hirt.

"Where is my wife?" Dimitri demanded, as did the other men. Hirt and the armed guards led us to one side of the room and pointed each one of us to our wives. My love, Angila, was frozen. She looked dead. Thoughts of revenge filled my head. I considered charging Hirt and killing him with my bare hands, but then I realized that the only way that I could be with Angila was to succumb. The other men concurred and we followed passively as we were led to the nurses' station by the elevator, eight floors above.

We took our places, each in a large, comfortable chair that reclined slightly. We were instructed to put in writing a description of everything that we recalled happening in the past couple of days, along with any specific medical instructions such as allergies and so forth. There were several pages of legal mumbo jumbo that I scanned, but my mind was too occupied with fear and anxiety to comprehend any of it, so I just signed where it required my signature.

Then we were briefed as to what was expected 0f us upon our awakening, but I recall very little that was said in that room. I was preoccupied with praying. I asked God to forgive me for my sins and to allow me to be with Angila once more. I remember hearing Dimitri say, just as the nurse injected a needle in my arm: "Good luck my friend, I hope to see you on the other side."

Chapter 18:
The LEM

My awakening was different this time. It wasn't cold like before, and the first sound that I heard was not Angila calling for me, but the sound of air rushing in and out, as if the ebb and flow of the ocean were sucking air in and out of a seaside cave. Angila *was* on my mind. I imagined that she and I were on a raft in the rough Pacific surf. We were trying desperately to overcome the strong current that was trying to smash us onto sharp rocks. We could feel the current pull us out to sea and then suddenly change directions. The rhythm of the current corresponded to the sound of the rushing wind. My dream faded as I became increasingly conscious. An unnatural sound, best described as a beeping noise, became increasingly noticeable. It had its own consistent rhythm. I opened my eyes and saw that a strange mask was covering part of my face, my nose, and my mouth. It had tubes made of a material that was unknown to me sprouting off in two different directions. There were doctors and nurses standing all around. I saw a computer for the first time. This was a very strange place that I had awakened to, but the strangest thing of all was that people seemed to communicate with one another without actually speaking.

The nurses knew what the doctor needed at just the right moment without a word being spoken. At the time, I thought that they were just well trained so verbal instructions were unnecessary.

A doctor removed the mask to examine my eyes, ears, and throat. I tried to speak, but my throat was too dry. As difficult as it was to speak, I managed to call for Angila. The doctor removed his green mask that matched his clothes, which I later learned were called scrubs, and smiled.

"Your wife, Angila, is alive and well. She is recovering in another room just like this one at this very moment," said the doctor.

A nurse placed a paper cup of water to my lips. My throat was temporarily soothed, but I could not speak.

"Mr. Cado, can you understand me? Nod your head if you can," I heard the doctor say.

I nodded my head but wasn't fully alert. The doctor could tell that I was bewildered, so he turned to a frail, silver-haired lady who suddenly appeared by my bedside.

"Mother, would you like to speak to your friend?" he spoke in Spanish.

She looked as if she were in her mid-eighties, but there was something familiar beyond her wrinkles. She placed her hand on mine affectionately and with a glimmer in her eyes, smiled.

"Welcome back, Johnny. Do you recognize me?" she asked, speaking in English.

Before answering, I looked about the room, still trying to comprehend where I was. When you first wake up from a freeze, there is a period of confusion, and it takes several minutes for your brain to process all of the information that is pouring in all at once. At that moment, I did not know where I was or how I got there. I shook my head slightly.

"No, I'm sorry," I said with a hoarse voice.

"That's understandable. I've changed a great deal after all of these years. I'm Zofia."

As if a fog had lifted, I realized that I had been frozen.

"How long?" I asked.

Zofia leaned closer and placed her hand on mine.

"My dear, this will come as a shock to you. Are you prepared?"

I nodded in affirmation.

"It's been one hundred years since we last spoke."

She gave me a few minutes to process that stunning information before continuing to speak. It was a good thing. My head swirled with questions.

"No, that's not possible," I replied.

"Yes, my dear, it is true, and the world today is vastly different than the world that you remember. In many ways it's better, but it can be very scary to someone who has not seen the advances in science and technology take place gradually over time as I have. But don't be afraid, I am here for you and Angila and also for Talia and Dimitri," she said reassuringly.

The old lady resembled Zofia, but her English was much improved, and the Zofia that I knew did not speak Spanish. I began to suspect deception.

"How are Angila and the others?" I asked.

"She is recovering well. I just left her room to check on you. The two of you will be together as soon as the doctors are comfortable that it is safe to move you into another room. That should happen in less than ten or fifteen minutes," she said with a gentle pat of her hand on mine.

"What happened? Where am I?"

"You were frozen in 1946. Now you are in the Berghof compound in the year 2046. As I said before, the world has advanced so much in the past one hundred years, some people are overwhelmed and cannot properly deal with the shock. It's very important to your mental health to be introduced to the changes at a pace that is suitable to you. Remember, you are the reason that I am here, to protect you, so don't be afraid."

"What is there to be afraid of?" I asked.

"The doctors have learned from experience that some people from your time are terrified by some of the technologies that we are accustomed to today. Think about how much changed from 1846 to 1946. No one in 1846 could imagine armored tanks, aircraft carriers, jet planes, or even a telephone or horseless carriage. Scientific advances have occurred far more rapidly in the past century, and you might find some things difficult to comprehend. It's best that you go through an orientation program to learn the progression of these advances in order to protect your mental health. You and Angila will do this together."

I'm certain that I still had a bewildered look on my face.

"How could a hundred years have passed? Why are they just now waking me up?"

"Angila, Talia, and Dimitri will have the same questions, so why not wait until you are all together?" the doctor said.

The doctor seemed like a friendly, good-natured person. He thanked Zofia for her assistance.

"I am so very pleased to meet you and am especially pleased that I was chosen to oversee your awakening," the doctor said.

"Allow me to introduce you to my son, John. You may remember him as little Giovanni," Zofia said, smiling and gesturing to the doctor.

"I want to thank you for saving my mother's life and mine," the doctor said before I could respond.

Clarity had returned to my mind by this time, and I realized that if a hundred years had passed, these two should be much older. I asked Zofia for an explanation.

"You may recall that the Nazis' plan was to freeze Hitler until a cure for his cancer could be discovered? Well, it has taken much longer for a cure than anyone had imagined, and we were frozen for a time also, but not as long as you. I lived here at the compound with John and Kam all this time. A cure was recently developed, so this is the week of what the Nazis call the great awakening. You and Angila were among the first to be awakened. They are in the process of awakening thousands of soldiers before awakening their Fuehrer, Adolf Hitler. Don't worry though, you and Angila will be set free, just as your contract with Hitler states. There is nothing to be concerned about," Zofia said.

"Angila will have all of the same questions and is waiting. Why don't we get the two of you together? I want you to sit up now, but go slow and easy. We will need to get your blood flowing to your lower extremities, but not too quickly," said Doctor John.

A nurse moved into place between Zofia and me so that she could assist Dr. John in helping me to sit upright. I hadn't noticed until now that I had a tube connected to a vein in my hand. They helped me to stand. After ensuring that I was stable, they led me and my IV pole out the door to a similar room on the opposite side of the hall. Angila was lying in her bed, connected to an IV just like me. The last time that I saw her, she was frozen and appeared dead. I was pleased when she turned her head toward me and smiled.

Her face seemed to brighten as I approached. I leaned over and gave her a hug and a kiss. Simultaneously we said to one another: "I love you," and we closed our eyes and silently thanked God for keeping us alive so that we could be together once again. Then I whispered into her ear so that no one else could hear.

"They are waking up Hitler in a matter of days. We have to get out of here before that happens."

Angila's doctor stepped closer. I suspected that he wanted to hear what I was whispering into her ear.

"Guess who that is?" Angila asked as she looked at her doctor. He was about the same age as Dr. John, but he did not look familiar to me.

The doctor extended his hand and introduced himself before I could speak.

"I'm Dr. Kam Nowak. Mother told me so much about you. I've waited most of my life for this day."

Kam was Kamila's baby, but he had Zofia's last name. She must have adopted Kam as her own. The thought of everyone that I knew having passed away or grown old caused a deep sense of sorrow. Kam could see from my expression that I was depressed.

"Are you feeling all right?" he asked.

I didn't answer him. I was lost in my thoughts of all of those years gone by. While everyone else was living life, I was sleeping in a deep-frozen coma.

Angila could see that I was sad also.

"Isn't it a wonderful blessing that Zofia and her boys are here for us?" she said in an attempt to lift my spirits.

I attempted to return the smile and nodded approvingly.

Kam opened a cabinet drawer and removed a bottle containing pills. He poured a couple of the pills into his hand and offered them to me along with a paper cup of water.

"Take these. They help with depression, which is not an uncommon side effect," he said.

Kam instructed everyone to give Angila and me some time to be alone, but Angila asked Zofia to remain.

This gave Zofia her first and only opportunity to warn us about the LEM. She explained that we had been "wired," meaning that we had been implanted with a small electronic device called a microchip that sends and receives radio signals wirelessly through something called the Internet. This was very confusing to Angila and me. We had seen a television only once before, while in Paris, and the quality of the broadcast was so poor, I didn't think that people would ever prefer one over a radio. We were one of the few who had a telephone in our home. Terms such as microchip and Internet were completely alien to us. Zofia could see from our facial expressions that we were confused.

"You will understand what I am telling you after you complete your orientation, but there are a couple of things that they will not tell you, so I will warn you now. You will be told about all of the benefits of having a LEM installed inside your body, but they won't tell you that the government can track your whereabouts, or that the LEM records everything that you see, hear, and say," she said.

She paused to evaluate our reactions before continuing with her warning.

"My dears, the most frightening thing about the LEM is that it can access your memories and project them for others to see. You need to hear this now, because your LEM has not been fully activated yet, but once you've completed orientation, the device will be activated. From that moment forward, you must be very careful what you say and do, because everything will be recorded. I would be in big trouble for telling you this, and they would know if I had a LEM," Zofia explained.

"Wait. You don't have a LEM? Why do we have to have one?" I asked.

"Argentinean law does not require everyone to have a LEM, and since I am a harmless old lady who has all of her living needs provided for her, the authorities here at the Berghof did not feel that the expense of installing a LEM in me was justified. However, the United States passed a law, years ago, requiring everyone to have a LEM installed."

She paused and offered water to Angila and I before continuing.

"This is the other thing that they will not tell you, and it's very important: there are differing levels of permissions that can be programmed into the LEM. In most parts of the world, such as in South America and in the European Union, citizens still have certain rights of privacy, so the government cannot access the information stored in your LEM without a court issuing a warrant based on probable cause, but that isn't the case in the United States. The American government passed a law years ago requiring everyone who receives government benefits to have a LEM installed, under the guise that it monitors a person's health and therefore saves lives. Soon the LEM replaced the need for debit cards, computers, and cell phones, which you will learn all about in orientation," Zofia explained.

We had no idea what any of those things were—something cards, computers, and cell phones were alien to us.

"You will also learn that the United States has been at war with Middle East Islamic terrorists groups for the past forty years. The attacks in American cities and towns started out with terrorists flying planes into buildings, killing thousands of innocent people, including women and children. Then random terror attacks on individuals across America took place," Zofia continued.

Angila looked at me with a bewildered expression. Zofia noticed our quizzical expressions, but continued explaining with a sense of urgency.

"Women were beheaded at the places they worked by coworkers who converted to Islam. Civil war broke out after an entire city was destroyed by what is known as a nuclear dirty bomb. That resulted in the president of the United States declaring martial law, and just like Abraham Lincoln, abolishing habeas corpus. The president became the dictator of the United States. Using the need to restore law and order and to protect Americans from terrorists, he issued an executive order requiring all Americans to have a LEM installed. The LEM allows citizens to be identified and makes it easier to identify and track suspected terrorists, all in the name of national security. This caused a huge exodus of Americans from the USA. Over twenty million Americans, referred to as ex-pats, moved to Argentina alone in the past twenty years. The only people left in America are those who are either dependent on government, work for the government, or cannot leave for one reason or another. The one-party dictatorship in the United States passed more laws taking away more and more of the rights of its citizens all in the name of protecting them from terrorists. The LEM can now be used to prevent crime by monitoring thoughts and causing a person to feel pain if they even consider breaking a law, or say the wrong thing. The American government has complete control over the population. Wouldn't Adolf Hitler love to rule such a country? Here is the final point that you need to know: the Nazis here at the Berghof have a plan to hack into the American government's computers and take control of the entire system. Whoever controls the government's computer system controls the American population. Once they have control of the government's computer, they plan to install Adolf Hitler as the supreme leader of the United States, and the world will be his in a matter of time," she said.

This was too much information for me to understand all at one time, and I felt helpless to do anything about any of it anyway, so I turned my thoughts to our personal situation.

"What do you propose that we do?" I asked.

"We need to warn someone," Angila said.

"As soon as you are physically able, you must escape this place. John and Kam will help you, but be careful that you do not say anything to them about what I've said. John and Kam have LEMs that are monitored by the Berghof officials. It will be best to escape before they fully activate your LEMs, because the Nazis will program your software as they see fit, which won't be good for you. We plan to send you off in a taxi with Talia and Dimitri, which will take you as far as San Carlos de Barilche. From there, you must make your way to the Italian embassy in Buenos Aires. You will not be safe in Argentina or America once Hitler is awakened."

"Why must we escape? I have a contract with Adolf Hitler," asked Angila.

"My sweet, dear Angila, have you never known of Adolf Hitler to lie or renege on a contract?" replied Zofia.

I began to feel anxious and despite my feebleness was ready to get the hell out of the Berghof.

"Why wait until the orientation? Let's get out of here now," I said.

"There are preparations that must be made first. As I explained, the LEM is not required by law in Argentina, but it is not practical to go without a LEM anywhere in the world, other than in some parts of Africa and the Middle East. At this moment, there is no way to prove who you are, and you have no money," said Zofia.

"What happened to our ten ounces of gold?" Angila asked.

"You have your gold coins, which can be converted to money, but you see dear, in order to buy things or hire someone to do something, you must have an electronic account which transfers money—we call them bitcoins—from your account to another's account. No one uses cash or coins any longer. Trying to move about the country would be nearly impossible, unless you find a charitable stranger. The war on terror will cause strangers to be wary of you, especially if you don't have an activated LEM to identify you. You see, most Islamic countries have banned the LEM, so anyone without one is automatically suspected of being a terrorist," she explained.

"This is all so complicated," Angila said.

"There is another consideration. As you walk along the street, your LEM is supposed to alert everyone within a certain range of your presence. The United States government has drones—mechanical things that look exactly like hummingbirds, mosquitos, and many other animals. Drones have recording devices designed to find terrorists all over the world by locating people who don't have LEMs installed."

"You've convinced us, we won't be going to America," I said.

"You have to be concerned about drones everywhere in the world, especially here in the Americas. The USA has no respect for the boundaries of other countries. The war on terror justifies everything for the Americans. Without a properly activated LEM, you will be picked up by the Americans in no time," she said.

"My God, what has the world come to?" This was more of statement than a question from Angila.

Once again, I felt as if the situation were completely hopeless. My depression deepened. I wanted to go back to sleep and wake up in another one hundred years, just in case things were to get better.

"Please, tell me what the plan is. Where do we go and how do we get there?" I asked.

"Argentina is still a democracy dedicated to individual liberties, but there are Nazi infiltrators throughout the country and in the government who will be notified by the Berghof once you leave here. The safest place on earth for you is Europe. During your orientation, your LEM will be programmed to identify you as Italian citizens living in

Argentina. This will suffice for the Argentinean officials, but it won't work for the Italian government. You must get to the Italians and claim that you are a kidnap victim whose LEM has been tampered with. The LEM will transmit a code that will prove your ancestry to the Italians, which should grant you asylum to Italy. Try to remember that if the Italian government asks you for permission to access your DNA, grant the permission."

"DNA?" I asked.

"I cannot explain DNA. It's too complicated. During orientation, you will learn how to get answers to any question in the world by accessing an Internet search engine through your LEM, but for now just remember to grant permission to any government that asks to access your DNA," Zofia answered.

"You sound as if you are speaking English, but talking a foreign language," Angila said.

"Dimitri and Talia should go to the German embassy and follow the same plan. You must get out of the Americas as soon as possible, because your knowledge of the Berghof is a danger to the Nazis' plan. I'm afraid that they have kept you alive only because of your contract with Hitler. John and Kam will create bank accounts for each of you and trade your gold for bitcoins. They will chip in a little extra for you from their accounts as well. Since I am the only one without a LEM, I will be the one to give you instructions as to what to do and when to do it," Zofia said.

"Tell the court about your so-called orientation."

Orientation was like being in school, but the teacher was a holographic image of Professor Hirt standing before us.

The first class lasted eight hours and provided us with a history lesson beginning with the fall of Germany, but from the Nazi point of view. Angila and I watched and listened to the Hirt hologram from our recovery room beds. We held hands most of the time. Subsequent lessons focused on technological advancements over time. It was fascinating, especially the past fifty years: the Internet, cell phones, 3-D printers, artificial skin, and artificial intelligence.

The subject of the final class was the LEM. The benefits were clear to see. The LEM monitors everything about your health and makes dietary recommendations based on your personal calorie and vitamin needs. Heart attacks had become far less common since the invention of the LEM, but if you did have one, emergency responders would be notified before you noticed any symptoms. The LEM all but destroyed the black market, because cash was eliminated and all transactions could be traced electronically. The LEM is a crime fighter. No one can sneak up behind you anymore, because the LEM will notify you, and if someone threatened you, your heart rate would alert authorities, who could instantly access the cameras that are everywhere and see what was happening. If Zofia hadn't warned us of the pitfalls of the LEM, I believe that I would have been a proponent of the LEM after watching the eight-hour propaganda promoting its benefits.

We learned new terminology that was prevalent in this new, strange world: things like right click, left click, double click, the Internet, the cloud, and Google. It was good to learn that everything we learned was recorded by our LEM and so could easily be retrieved for review. The most fascinating thing was the fact that I had access to all of the information in the history of the world by simply utilizing a search engine called Google, or a site called Wikipedia. It was almost too fantastic to believe.

The hologram of Professor Hirt disappeared instantly at the conclusion of our orientation, and the room became brighter from the ceiling light. Hans, Kam, and a man named Jorge entered the room.

"It's time to begin programming your LEM with your unique number and bar code so that you will be properly identified. There is a problem with your dates of birth. If we show your actual dates of birth, the authenticity of your LEM with be questioned. We are going to list your dates of birth to be one hundred years later—for example, Angila was born in the year 2015 and Johnny in 1999. The problem with this is that there are no records of your birth anywhere to verify this information, which will be difficult to explain to the authorities if questioned," Jorge said.

I wondered if this were the time to attempt an escape, but Zofia was not in the room to provide instruction.

"There is nothing to be afraid of at this time," Kam said, apparently recognizing my apprehension.

Jorge pulled my bed away from the wall so that he could stand behind me. He placed his hands on both sides of my head and used his fingers to close the tragus on each ear.

"Relax, you won't feel a thing," Jorge said.

He opened and closed each tragus in a methodical pattern, which I later learned programmed my LEM.

"Do you see that?" Jorge asked.

"What?" I asked.

"There should be a screenshot of numbers and symbols that you see before you," he answered.

I had not noticed before, but images of numbers and symbols had appeared in front of me and seemed to float suspended in the air inches away from my face. I reached to touch the image, but the display seemed to float out of reach. The image followed my vision as I glanced around the room. Jorge instructed me how to use my vision and thoughts to select numbers and symbols that appeared in the floating display before me. My LEM was now programmed. Jorge repeated the process with Angila.

Jorge instructed Angila to send a text message to me, using nothing more than her thoughts. I heard a pleasant tone and felt a slight vibration behind my right ear. As instructed, I clicked my right tragus, which displayed my text messages. Using my eyes, I moved the curser to the message from Angila. In order to open the message to read, I had the option of clicking my right tragus, or I could focus my eyes on the message and think the word "click." I tried the latter and it worked. Angila's message opened, and I saw the words and simultaneously heard her voice say: "I will love you forever." No one else could see the imagery before me, unless I selected and clicked the option to allow others to see the message. I kept the conversation private and prepared my reply, which was "I will love you more forever." The LEM notified me that the spell check was complete and the message was ready to send. This was a fascinating experience. We could carry on a conversation in any language without using our vocal cords.

Jorge taught us how to make a telephone call to one another by opening our address book and instructing the LEM to make the call. My ear vibrated differently from before, alerting me that Angila was calling. I answered with a click to my left tragus. This time, we had to use our vocal cords to speak to one another, but I learned that we could reach each other this way no matter where we were in the entire world. This is a strange new world we live in.

EXTERNAL EAR

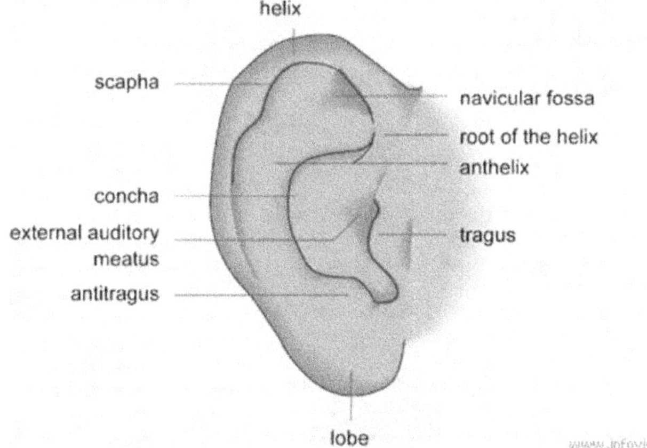

Once satisfied that we could navigate our way around the LEM to communicate, utilize search engines, and access our medical records and our one and only bank account, Jorge recommended that we be left alone to practice our new computer skills.

"Would it be all right if Zofia visited?" Angila asked politely.

"I see no reason to object," replied Jorge.

Zofia and Kam returned within an hour. Kam was carrying a couple of bags and placed one on each of our beds.

"Get dressed in these clothes. It is time to act," Zofia said as she pointed to the bags.

Kam looked away respectfully as Angila and I stood and dropped our hospital gowns. We got dressed in the clothes provided: blue jeans and cotton shirts. Zofia explained that we must not try to speak to message Kam or John while in range of the Berghof, for the LEM would record the communication and cause big trouble later.

Zofia would do all of the talking.

"We have a taxi waiting outside for you. John will bring Talia and Dimitri there to join you. Follow Kam and don't say a word to either Kam or John until they give you clearance. They may say something to you, likely in code, but you are not to respond verbally," Zofia explained.

"Please come with us," Angila said to Zofia.

"My sweet Angila. I love you as the sister that I never had, but I am old and will slow you down. Besides, my boys are here. I will never leave them, but you have my love. I did not tell you before, but I agreed to be frozen so that I could be here with you on this very day. Now go. Get away and live a happy life, or my efforts will have been for nothing," Zofia said just before she hugged Angila and kissed her on the cheek. Then she turned to look at me.

"You take good care of my big sister."

"You have my word," were the last words that I spoke to the loyal Zofia.

We followed Kam down the hall past other workers and guards who seemed oblivious to our presence. We passed a lot of recovery rooms filled with patients. I recalled that this was the week that the Germans were thawing ten thousand Nazi disciples, culminating with the thawing of Adolf Hitler.

The elevator doors opened automatically as we approached. Without saying a word, Kam instructed the elevator to descend. The elevator doors opened once more, this time revealing a new level that I had not seen before. We followed the hall to an exit door. The exit door's sensors recognized Kam and opened automatically to the wonderfully cold, open air and sky above the compound's employee parking lot. We were outside the compound for the first time in over one hundred years!

We walked past rows of strange-looking parked cars to the awaiting taxi. The doors responded to Kam's silent request and opened, allowing us to take our seats. There were three rows of seats, providing room for six passengers. Angila and I sat in the back seats. Kam sat in a front-row seat. We waited impatiently for about ten minutes until John arrived with Talia and Dimitri. John joined Kam in the front. Talia and Dimitri filled the remaining middle-row seats. The car's engine started. Mechanical arms extended on each side of the car, and propellers began to twirl. To my surprise we took off straight up into the air like a helicopter! Once clear of the compound, the arms repositioned to the front of the car in such a way that we stopped climbing and began to fly forward. I could see the Berghof disappearing in the distance behind us. Angila and I kissed. We thought that this must be the end of the nightmare that we had been living. Once we were far outside of the Berghof's electronic monitoring range, Kam and John began to talk.

"This taxi can go only where it is preprogrammed, so it will drop us off at a grocery store where we shop regularly. Once there, we will go our separate ways. Access the Internet, as you were taught, to locate a rental car company to take to Buenos Aires. Driving is simple. You simply give the car the address of where you want to go and then sit back and relax. The car does all the driving and flying for you," said John.

"What will happen to Zofia and you and Kam?" Angila asked.

"Nothing will happen to us. No one will suspect Kam or me because we've been loyal to the Fourth Reich, as far as anyone else knows. They won't suspect mother because she is so old and feeble. You have our numbers programmed in your contact book. Call us when you are safely in Europe, but remember, do not say anything incriminating, for we will still be in danger on our side of the Atlantic," John answered.

The flying car landed in a grocery store parking lot. Directly across the street was a sand beach that made the shore of the beautiful Nahuel Huapi Lake. We expressed our heartfelt thanks to John and Kam before saying goodbye. They entered the grocery store to complete the deception, and the four of us walked as free people for the first time in a very long time.

"I recommend that we find a pub so that we can sit down and drink a beer, while we search online for a rental car," Dimitri suggested.

"That is a great idea. We look like lost tourists here. The sooner that we can get out of plain sight, the better," I concurred.

We began walking along the road that followed the lake's shoreline toward an area where we heard music and the sound of revelers. I felt more alive and free with each step. The temperature was so much more pleasant at this elevation than we had experienced in the mountains. I took in the sites as we walked. The trees and vegetation were so beautiful, as were the buildings.

There were people on the beach enjoying the warm sun. I imagined this one couple, lying on a blanket in the sand, was Angila and me. I could hear sounds that I hadn't heard in a very long time, such as the sound of birds chirping and whistling. I noticed this one pretty bird sitting on the rail that separated the sidewalk from the beach. It had beautiful feathers and big, black, strange-looking eyes that stared at us as we walked by. I recalled Zofia's warning about American drones disguised as birds, so I turned quickly and reached out to grab the bird, but it was too quick for me. It flew up about fifteen feet into the air and landed on the rail about twenty feet ahead of us.

"Leave that bird alone, sweetheart. It's done nothing to you," Angila said sweetly.

The bird continued staring at us as we walked by. It did not fly away even when I was close to it, just beyond arm's length. Once we were well past it, the bird flew past us and landed on the rail before us once more. I was obsessed with the bird and was determined to catch it the next time it was within arm's reach. When that time came, I pounced to grab the bird with two hands, but once again it was too fast for me.

Dimitri laughed.

"Oh my, Johnny is determined to capture that bird," Talia said.

"Honey, what is it with that bird?" Angila asked.

The bird landed on top of a nearby street lamp, well beyond my reach. I composed a group text message to Angila, Talia, and Dimitri and sent the warning:

"That bird does not appear to be a real bird. Its eyes look more like little cameras. I think we are under surveillance."

"OK," was Angila's simple reply via text.

The others did not respond. They thought I was paranoid. I forgot about the bird once we made our way into a crowd that had gathered to watch an entertainer juggle flaming knives. Children were eating cotton candy. I thought about how lucky these people were to have seemingly normal lives.

San Carlos de Barilche

We found a pub that had several empty chairs at the bar and a couple of empty tables. The sign read: "Please seat yourself," so we chose a table where we would be unlikely to engage in conversation with a stranger. No sooner had we sat than text appeared in front of my eyes asking me if I wanted a menu. I selected "yes" and "click," which resulted in a menu being displayed before me. The prices were shocking. It would take a week's wages from my day to purchase one beer, but after one taste of the beer, I no longer had any complaints.

"According to the Internet, there are several car rental companies just a few miles away on the edge of town," Dimitri said.

"Let's drink this one beer and go. I want to get as far away from this terrible place as possible as soon as possible," Angila said.

"Yes, please," Talia said in agreement.

"Should we try to find a taxi to take us to the car rental store, or should we walk?" Dimitri asked.

"Taxi, it's quicker," Talia answered.

"If we call for a taxi, the car will identify us, which might lead the Nazis from Berghof to us. Let's walk. Once we are in the rental car, we will have a big head start, even if they come after us," I reasoned.

They agreed, so we chugged our beers and followed the GPS instructions toward our destination, which was six miles outside of the city limits, a ten-mile walk in total. Half way to our destination, I saw that damn bird again.

"Look, there is that thing that looks like a bird. It's following us," I texted the group.

"Yes, I believe you now," Dimitri replied to the group text message.

"What should we do?" texted Talia.

"Keep calm; don't panic. I will think of something," I replied.

"That's comforting," Dimitri replied to the group text and then smiled at me.

"Very funny," I replied.

His humor helped relieve the tension of the moment and was much appreciated. We tried to ignore the fact that the bird kept following us for the next several miles. The first rental car store was within eyesight when suddenly two flying vans appeared seemingly from nowhere. One landed in front of us, and the other landed behind us. From each van sprang soldiers dressed in camouflage uniforms and helmets. I noticed their American flag shoulder patches and feared the worst. They instructed us to go with them, separating Talia and Dimitri from Angila and me. Angila forced herself free and ran to hug Talia. I tried to break free to protect Angila from the retaliation that I feared but was taken to the ground by two soldiers. The girls managed to hug one another so tightly that the soldiers had difficulty separating them, but they did. My heart sank when I saw the tears streaming down the women's faces. I tried to send Dimitri a text message, but received an instant reply that said: "Message undeliverable, you are in American custody."

The soldiers pushed our heads down forcefully so that we would not bang our head on the flying van's doorframe. We were airborne within seconds.

"Will someone tell me what this is all about?" I demanded.

The soldiers did not answer. I looked at Angila, who sat facing me.

"Baby, I am so sorry—" I was interrupted with a painful shock that jolted through my body.

The flying van flew for several hours over land and eventually over the Atlantic Ocean, toward an awaiting aircraft carrier. I had never seen a ship of this magnitude and was in awe, even under the circumstances. We were handcuffed upon exiting the flying car onto the aircraft carrier's deck. A naval officer approached.

"You are aboard the USS *Barack Obama* and in the custody of the United States Navy. You are suspected of planning terrorist attacks on the United States. You will be transported to a nondisclosed location on American soil and questioned. If evidence is found to substantiate our suspicions, you will be charged with aiding and abetting an enemy of the United States of America during a time of war," the naval officer stated.

"May I speak?" Angila asked.

The officer hesitated but after hearing Angila's soft voice and seeing her kind face felt compelled to break with protocol and allow her to ask one question.

"We haven't harmed anyone, and neither one of us would ever harm a flea. We just want to go home and make babies," she said.

This was the first time that she had openly expressed that she was ready to have a baby. We were so close to being free, back there on the beach, but I blew it again. Maybe we should have taken a taxi to the car rental store after all.

"That is not what the evidence indicates, ma'am," the officer replied.

We were led to a jet plane that was ready for takeoff. Our handcuffs were removed before we climbed aboard. Once our seat belts were fastened, our hands were recuffed, and helmets were placed on our heads. The jet's engine roared, and we took off with a force like nothing that I've ever imagined before. The jet dipped as it flew off the end of the aircraft carrier, causing me to think that we were going to crash into the ocean, but soon we were above the clouds. Our LEMs were disabled, so Angila and I could not communicate via text or telephone.

The jet landed in Guantanamo, Cuba, where we were detained and questioned for two days. Angila and I were separated immediately, so we weren't able to agree on what to say in this case. I felt as if the truth would be too unbelievable, so I stuck with the lie that I was born in 1999 and had lived in Argentina as a rancher's hand all these years. My LEM didn't support that fabrication though, despite the fact that the Germans at the Berghof had told me that it would. As a result, I was charged with crimes against humanity, terrorism, and accessory to murder.

Chapter 19:
The Verdict

"That is how I came to be here today, pleading for my freedom and for my wife's and friend's freedoms."

"This is an interesting story, but how is it that your LEM is telling a different story today from when you were arrested?" asked the prosecutor.

"Our German captors at the Berghof were clever enough to plan for the possibility that we might escape. They programmed our LEMs to have a false memory, so that if we were captured by the authorities, there would be no evidence of Hitler or the Berghof. Instead, there would be fabricated evidence that we were in Argentina on behalf of an Islamic terrorist group, planning an attack on American interests. The CIA's bird drone hacked into our LEM's memory and determined that we were terrorists on the loose.

"But the Germans failed to take into consideration two very important facts: that the LEM and its software were invented in the USA, which has smarter engineers, and that I am Sicilian."

"Explain to the court what that means."

"Well first of all, the publicity about this trial caught the attention of some prominent Italian Americans, and they visited me in jail. When I told them my story, the real story, and that you assholes had confiscated all of my money because you claimed it was terrorist money, so I couldn't afford an attorney, they decided to help. They hired a computer software guru who was able to break the firewall—or something like that. Anyway, the bogus history that the Nazis planted in my LEM has been replaced, and the testimony that I've presented to this court is the result of my LEM tapping into my brain's memory."

"Who is the prominent Italian American? Can he corroborate this testimony?"

"He is sitting right there next to my public defender and the Italian ambassador to the United States. His name is Senator Paul Marcello from right here in New York."

The public defender acknowledge that my testimony was true and correct. The senator stood and also confirmed for the court that my testimony was true.

The prosecutor's shoulders drooped as if he were defeated.

"I have no more questions, your honor. I rest my case."

My public defender stood up to make his case in my defense. He reminded the court that the Constitution of the United States had been amended to allow for courts to use the memory of defendants, as recorded by a LEM, to replace the jury of peers, and that the Supreme Court had upheld the amendment as being constitutional. He followed that point with the argument that I was not a citizen of the United States but was a citizen of Italy. I was born in Sicily and immigrated with my mother to New Orleans when I was ten, but I never applied to become an American citizen. I considered myself an American, but legally I was an Italian. My defender also pointed out that I had not been charged with any crimes that occurred within the jurisdiction of the United States.

"Any crimes that the defendant may or may not have committed in the United States, would have been so long ago that the statute of limitations would have expired long ago, for Johnny Cado has not been in the United States for over one hundred years," the young defender argued.

It worried me that I had to accept a public defender, because my perception was that only the worst lawyers would work for peanuts, but this guy had talent.

"Furthermore, the defendant was unlawfully kidnapped to be put on trial here. The American agreement with Argentina does not apply to Italians who might be living in or visiting Argentina, and no agreement is in place for Americans to arrest Italians abroad. For these reasons, I demand that this case be dismissed and the defendant to be turned over to the Italian government," the public defender continued.

The three judges whispered among themselves.

"Does the Italian government recognize Mr. Cado's citizenship?" asked the African American judge who sat in the center of the three judges.

The Italian ambassador stood.

"Yes, your honor. I have Mr. and Mrs. Cado's passports with me if you care to see," he answered.

"In that case, we shall take a short recess and return with a verdict momentarily. Do not leave the courtroom," she said.

"All rise!" said the bailiff in a commanding voice.

I stepped down from the witness chair and took my seat next to my attorney. The senator put his hand on my shoulder to get my attention.

"Mr. Cado, there will be a lot of interest in your story. Do you mind if I have a publisher friend of mine contact you? I think that it would be good for you to know him," said Senator Marcello.

"Sure. Give him my number. I owe you so much, thank you," I replied.

The judges returned to the courtroom.

"All rise!"

We stood until the judges were seated and the bailiff gave permission to sit.

"Mr. Cado, I find you to be a despicable person. You are a racist, a thug, and I believe you are a killer. You admitted that you voluntarily belonged to one of history's most violent criminal organizations, the Italian Mafia," the black judge said.

This was not the response that I had expected. The confidence that I had felt moments ago quickly left me.

"I believe that you belong in jail, but there is no proof that you are an American citizen—and there is no tangible proof of any crimes. The only proof is your memory, which could be a counterfeit creation of some computer programmer that you've hired, so this court has no choice but to turn you over to the Italian government. But Mr. Cado, do not ever return to the United States. Case dismissed," the judge said as she slammed her gavel.

The courtroom erupted in applause.

"Your honor, I move that the case against Mrs. Angila Cado be dismissed also," yelled the public defender over the loud courtroom.

"The case for Angila Cado is dismissed also," she said.

After the trial, Angila and I were given Italian passports, but before relocating to the land of our birth, we traveled first to Panama. Talia and Dimitri were waiting for us in the hotel lobby of the Waldorf Astoria. The choice of the hotel was mine, but there was no resemblance to the old Waldorf Astoria that I remembered back in New York.

The sensors on the hotel's doors recognized us from the wireless signal transmitted from the LEM implanted in our bodies. We heard the automated voice welcome each one of us by name, as the doors opened before us and closed behind us. We walked through the lobby and past the front desk. The familiar tone alerted me that I had an incoming message. I clicked my left tragus once, which displayed a list of messages before my eyes. Using the movement of my eyes, I selected the one new message, which was from the Waldorf Astoria Panama and clicked my left tragus once more. The voice of a pleasant-sounding woman was transmitted from my LEM to be heard in my mind, as realistic as if a real person had been next to me.

"Welcome to the Waldorf Astoria Panama, Mr. Cado. We hope that you enjoy your stay. You've been checked into room number 1224, which is on the twelfth floor. Do you need directions to the elevator?"

An image illuminated before me, providing me with options to answer yes, no, or back. I selected no.

"Thank you. You may proceed to your room. Enjoy your stay," said the automated voice.

Talia and Dimitri saw Angila and me standing at the hotel's front desk and rushed to give us welcoming hugs. It was a joyous reunion.

"Come, my friend, I will show you to your room. I've taken care of everything, so no need to check in with the hotel," said Dimitri.

"We can check in later. I'm starved. Let's eat," I said.

"I know just the place," I said.

The Waldorf Astoria Panama

We left our luggage with the hotel's bellhop, and asked the concierge to arrange for a taxi. Within minutes we were in a flying taxi on our way to La Ristorante Italiano, which had been one of my favorites when I lived in Panama before. I was surprised that it was still in business. I had another reason for going there. Panama had changed so much in one hundred years, I needed a reference point that I was familiar with in order to find my old beach house and the Banco de Panama where my money had been deposited.

The driverless flying taxi took us directly to our destination. We took our seats and placed our orders via our individual holographic displays.

Dimitri explained that the verdict in our trial was used to get the cases against him and Talia dismissed, and the German ambassador had come to his defense, producing German passports just as the Italian ambassador had done for us.

I announced my plan to keep my promise to Dimitri. We were to open up a restaurant together with the money that I had in the Panamanian bank.

We searched unsuccessfully for the bank, but it was no longer in business. Other bankers told us that in the 1980s the Panamanian government had seized bank accounts that they deemed to be funded by questionable sources, or which had had no activity for many years. It was likely that my funds had been confiscated during that decade.

My beach house was also gone. In its place was a high-rise resort hotel. The trip to Panama was unsuccessful. We left without finding my money or any proof that I owned the valuable real estate where the resort was located. To make matters worse, the trip was expensive: it took nearly a third of my total bitcoin account to pay for our airline tickets and hotel rooms.

Angila and I decided to go to Sicily to see if either of us had distant relatives who might be interested in helping us start a new life. Dimitri and Talia had no living relatives in Germany, so they elected to travel to Italy with us.

The long flights to and from Panama gave me time to become more familiar with my LEM. I wanted that thing out of me so that no one could access my private thoughts and activities or monitor my whereabouts, but since there wasn't anything that I could do about it at that moment, I decided to use it to explore what happened to all of the people from my past, via the fascinating world wide web. I couldn't find a thing about Mama or Melissa, but I learned the rest of the story regarding Katie and Ella.

Katie was sentenced to death and hanged by the Nazis for her role in helping British airmen escape occupied France. Ella told her story in a book, and in it said that among Katie's last words were for Ella to not to cry for her. "I won. I beat the Germans one hundred and fifty to one," she said, referring to the number of airmen's lives that were spared as the result of her sacrifice. Since America had not entered the war yet, Ella, being an American, was spared the death penalty, for her role in the French Underground. She was eventually exchanged for a German spy in a deal struck by the Nazis with America.

Carlos eventually became the boss of New Orleans and was even implicated in having a role in the assassination of a United States President. One theory is that Carlos wanted revenge after the CIA had kidnapped him off the street in New Orleans, flew him down to Guatemala, and dropped him off in the middle of the jungle. Carlos had to make his way through the jungle wearing an expensive dress suit and shoes to find his way back to civilization. To make matters worse, the CIA had taken his wallet, so not only did Carlos not speak Spanish; he had no money or identification. Despite all of that, he made his way back to New Orleans. Who could blame Carlos for being pissed at the President for ordering the CIA to do that to him?

Lucky eventually became the most powerful mafia boss of all time. With Meyer Lansky serving as his advisor, he devised the plan to organize crime. As a result, the leaders of the five families of New York along with the bosses of Chicago and Buffalo formed a board of directors or the Commission, which unified their efforts to make money in a variety of illegal ways and ended the Mafia wars for more than a decade. His new structure was such that the bosses were far removed from the people who actually committed the crimes, making it virtually impossible for the cops to pin anything on them. So, the cops fabricated evidence in order to convict him for running a prostitution ring. He was in prison when Angila and I were captives of the Nazis. Lucky was released from jail early for helping the Navy during World War II, by ordering his union-controlled longshoremen to help keep the docks safe from German sabotage. He also ordered Sicilians to cooperate with the

Americans during the invasion of Italy, which they did. The government wouldn't let Lucky stay in America though. He was exiled to Italy, where he died years later from a heart attack.

Meyer Lansky was smart enough to operate in the shadows and stay out of the papers. As a result, he died a natural death as a wealthy, old man who never spent a day in jail. During his lifetime, he was arguably the most powerful man in the underworld after Lucky was arrested, and even before then. He was able to attend Commission meetings, despite not being Italian. He couldn't vote, but he was very influential. In fact, some theorize that the entire mafia structure, including the Commission, was his idea.

Ben "Bugsy" Siegel is credited for being the brainchild behind the Flamingo Hotel and Casino which launched Las Vegas into the premier adult destination resort in the world. Siegel made the fatal mistake of involving his girlfriend in the business. Money came up missing and Siegel's girlfriend was blamed, but since Siegel was responsible, the Commission ordered the hit that ended his life. His lifelong best friends, Meyer Lansky and Lucky Luciano almost certainly approved of his assassination.

Frank Costello was running things as the Luciano Family's acting boss for Lucky while he was in jail, until Vito Genovese returned from exile and tried to assassinate Frank. Vito's hit man fired a shot at close range, but Costello's head was only grazed. It was enough to convince him that it was time to retire, so he struck a deal among Vito and Lucky which resulted in Vito taking over the Luciano Family, which has been known as the Genovese Family ever since. Frank died years later of natural causes.

Vito Genovese had gunmen kill Albert Anastasia while he was getting shaved by a public barber. His arrogance eventually exposed the mafia to the public. He ordered the mafia bosses and many of their top lieutenants to attend a national crime convention in upstate New York in order to pay homage to the new Boss of Bosses. During the meeting, a state trooper noticed an unusual number of late model cars with out of town and state license plates and called for backup to investigate. Over three hundred Mafioso were there from all over the country which confirmed that there was indeed a national organization controlling the various criminal empires. This led to one thing after another, but eventually, this is the single most devastating event which led to the mafia's ultimate downfall.

Heinrich Himmler was caught while trying to flee Germany. While in British captivity, a doctor conducted a medical exam on him. The doctor attempted to examine the inside of Himmler's mouth, but he jerked his head away. Himmler then bit into a hidden cyanide pill, invented by Sigmund Rascher, and collapsed onto the floor. He was dead within fifteen minutes.

Professor August Hirt, Hans Fischer aka Scarface, Adolf Hitler, and Eva Braun were never found after the end of the war, but we now know where they are.

The trip to Sicily was no better than Panama. We couldn't find any living relatives. Things seemed very bleak for the four of us. We were running out of money and would soon be broke and homeless.

Chapter 20:
The Picket Fence

Talia approached the bar and placed her order ticket for table number four on the spindle next to the chef's window: veal scaloppini, lasagna, one Peroni, and a glass of the house Cabernet.

Dimitri examined the order briefly, returned it to the spindle, and began preparing the food.

I was browsing through my social media and reading the headlines of the day.

"America's President Hitler announced that his new space-based weapon that harnesses the sun's energy can kill every man, woman, plant, and animal in its path at the speed of light. The death zone can be as small as a basketball or as wide as a small country. Hitler claims that nuclear weapons are obsolete because his space-based weapons circling earth are computer programmed to blast nuclear missiles within seconds of their launch," the reporter announced.

"My friend, you should go home and to be with your children or finish writing your book," Dimitri said.

Business was slow at this time of day, and I knew that Talia could pour drinks and open beer as well as me and still provide quality service to the customers.

"Good advice, my friend," I replied.

I walked around from behind the bar and spoke to the customers before leaving. The restaurant's door opened onto a wooden deck, which gave customers an opportunity to dine outdoors. I stood there for a moment and admired the view of the beach and the sea. I slipped off my shoes to walk through the sand past quaint little beachside shops, until I saw Angila on the beach playing with our two beautiful children, Cicero and Maria, and Talia and Dimitri's beautiful girls, Zofia and Kamila. Maria was the oldest at five years old, and Cicero was the youngest at just two years old.

Angila and I embraced one another as if we hadn't seen each other in a long time. The children laughed and made silly sounds when we kissed, but that didn't matter. We whispered to each other in the old-fashioned way with real words.

"I love you and will love you forever," she said, and I repeated it.

Then, as was our usual custom, we closed our eyes and thanked God for seeing us through all of the difficult times and providing us with the blessings that we now had: each other, our children, our beautiful home on the beach in San Vincenzo, and the restaurant that we owned together with Dimitri and Talia—The Picket Fence.

I hugged each and every child and told them that I loved them too. Then, I turned and opened the gate and passed through our own white picket fence. I stopped on the front porch, next to the porch swing, turned and looked back at my beautiful Angila, and thanked God once more.

My office is in the front of the house, where I can sit and watch my family play on the beach or swing on our porch swing. It is here that I do my best writing, and writing is what I must do. After all, I owe all of these wonderful blessings to that moment on the train from Rome, when God answered my prayer.

We had decided that if we were to be broke and homeless, it would be better to be in Northern Italy, where people are friendlier and towns are safer. We purchased train tickets from Rome to Florence, with Venice as our destination. I observed Talia and Dimitri, snuggled together in each other's arms, and realized that between the four of us, we did not have one single living relative on the planet. We were virtually broke, homeless, and alone. Despite all that Angila had been through since she had met me that fateful day in Sicily, she still loved me, and she still had faith in God above. She saw that I was worried.

"My darling, do not worry, God will take care of us. Close your eyes and pray, and he will answer," she said.

I don't know or care if you believe in God, but I can tell you that Angila and I have been to hell and back and survived. We hit the bottom and almost gave up, thinking that we would be better off dead, but now we thrive. I believe that without our love for one another and our faith in a higher power, we would not have survived our terrible journey. I closed my eyes and prayed as Angila instructed, and no sooner had I said amen, than a familiar vibration alerted me to an incoming call. It was from Senator Marcello's friend, the publisher. He offered to provide me with a generous advance for the exclusive right to my story, and I agreed. He transferred the money to my account while we were still on the train. The next stop was San Vincenzo. Angila and I took that as a sign from God, so we got off the train with Talia and Dimitri and made this beautiful seaside resort town our home. The money from book sales was nice, but the money from the movie was even better. I've been able to keep all of my promises, and for that I am eternally thankful. With that said, the final chapter of my book, *Unlucky Double,* is complete.

Support starving artists—book reviews beget more sales

Please be kind and review this book.

For more books by Darryl Breland Visit:

http://dbreland.wix.com/darrylbreland

or

The "My Books" page at

www.Breland.biz